Two Steps Back

by Belle Payton

Simon Spotlight

New York   London   Toronto   Sydney   New Delhi

SIMON SPOTLIGHT
An imprint of Simon & Schuster Children's Publishing Division
1230 Avenue of the Americas, New York, New York 10020
This Simon Spotlight edition March 2015
© 2015 by Simon & Schuster, Inc. All rights reserved, including the right of reproduction in whole or in part in any form.
SIMON SPOTLIGHT and colophon are registered trademarks of Simon & Schuster, Inc.
Text by Sarah Albee
Cover art by Anthony VanArsdale
For information about special discounts for bulk purchases, please contact Simon & Schuster Special Sales at 1-866-506-1949 or business@simonandschuster.com.
Designed by Ciara Gay
The text of this book was set in Garamond.
Manufactured in the United States of America 0215 OFF
10 9 8 7 6 5 4 3 2 1
ISBN 978-1-4814-2518-6 (pbk)
ISBN 978-1-4814-2519-3 (hc)
ISBN 978-1-4814-2520-9 (eBook)
Library of Congress Catalog Card Number 2014935214

CHAPTER ONE

"Hello? Yes, this is Alexandra Sackett." Alex put her hand to her right ear to muffle the sounds of the food court. "Yes. I—I did? I *did*? Oh my gosh, thank you! Yes! Yes! Yes, I will! Thank you! Bye!" She clicked off her phone and stared at it in disbelief.

Her friend Emily Campbell had paused in mid-sip of her raspberry smoothie. "What's going on, Alex? Who was that?"

Alex clutched her phone with both hands as though she expected it to leap away from her. "I won," she said quietly. "I *won*?" Her voice grew stronger. "I *won*!"

"That is so awesome!" squealed Emily,

bouncing up and down in her chair. "Congratulations! Um, what did you win?"

Alex took a breath and composed herself. She looked at her friend, her green eyes shining. "That was the assistant to Marcy Maxon, the TV reporter."

"Marcy Maxon! I totally know who that is! She's a celebrity! Why did her assistant call you?"

"I won the essay contest, Em! The one for KHXA's 'Tomorrow's Reporters Today' series? I wrote an essay, and Marcy Maxon's assistant just told me that I was selected to be a kid reporter. I get to write, produce, and star in a feature story, and it's going to air next Sunday night! She said to check my e-mail, because they'll be sending me all the details."

"Alex, that is absolutely and completely amazing!" said Emily. "Everyone in Ashland watches that segment! I've never known any of the kids who've done it, though. I can't believe I know you!"

Alex beamed at her friend. She loved that Emily seemed so genuinely happy for her, and it was fun to hear Emily's enthusiastic words in her pretty Texan drawl. Ever since Emily's best friend, Lindsey Davis, had started spending most of her time with her boyfriend, Alex and Emily had grown even closer.

Emily leaped out of her chair and came around the table to give Alex a big congratulatory hug.

"What are we celebrating?" asked a voice behind them.

Alex slackened her grip on Emily and turned to see who it was. She gasped with surprise.

Luke Grabowski was standing right there between their table and the smoothie counter. He looked impossibly gorgeous in a faded black T-shirt and khaki shorts. Behind him were two of his friends that Alex didn't know. The three of them were holding paper cups from a fancy coffee place across the way, and Luke had a book under one arm. *Of course he has a book with him,* Alex thought. He was not just beautiful; he was also smart. And funny. And nice. In short, perfect.

Luke was her twin sister Ava's tutor. Alex had had a crush on him from the moment she'd first met him, but no one in the world knew it, she was positive. Well, except maybe Emily and Lindsey, because she might have mentioned to them that she had been talking to a high school boy—she couldn't help gushing a little!

"Oh, hi!" she said, but her voice came out all squeaky. She didn't dare look into his gorgeous blue eyes, so instead she focused her gaze on the coffee he was holding. Drinking coffee was such a high school thing. She'd never really liked it much, but she immediately resolved to add "try coffee again" to her to-do list.

"So did you guys just win the lottery?" Luke prompted. "We heard the squealing across the food court."

Alex giggled. She raised her eyes to look at Luke, and then quickly looked away, overcome with bashfulness. She wasn't usually at a loss for words. On the contrary, Ava often told her she talked way too much and too quickly, but there was something about being in the presence of a crush that made her shy and awkward. And Luke was simply too handsome to look at for too long. It was like staring at the sun or something. But she recovered enough to introduce Emily.

"Nice to meet you, Emily," Luke said, his voice as smooth as melted chocolate. "And this is Pete, and that's Brandon. We were just loading up on caffeine before we hit the books." He held up his cup of coffee. "But tell us what the big celebration is all about," he said.

"Oh, ha-ha," said Alex. "It's no big deal." She tried not to blush, although she knew she must be turning the same shade as Emily's smoothie.

Emily stepped up and saved her. "No big deal? Yeah, right! It's a *huge* deal! I was congratulating Alex because she just won an essay contest! She's going to be a kid reporter for KHXA. Marcy Maxon's *assistant* just called her!"

"Wow!" said Luke. He put an arm around Alex's shoulder and gave her a little squeeze. She gulped.

"Awesome!" said Brandon.

Alex felt herself flush even more deeply. She couldn't think of a thing to say, but she knew that it was her turn to speak. Her eyes landed on Luke's coffee. "So, um, how's your coffee?" she asked. *Lame, lame, lame. What a dumb, stupid, idiotic question.*

"I haven't tried it yet," said Luke. He took a sip and made a face. "It's actually awful," he said, after swallowing with difficulty. "I think they gave me someone else's order. It tastes like there's pumpkin spice or something in here. They put pumpkin in everything this time of year!"

"I love pumpkin spice!" said Alex quickly, and

5

then mentally kicked herself. What if he thought that was babyish or something?

"Here, have it then," said Luke, handing his cup to her with an easy grin. "I'll pick up a more manly drink on my way out."

"Thanks!" said Alex. *Say something, say anything, keep the conversation going.* "So, are you enjoying the book you're reading?" she asked.

"What book? Oh, this?" He held it up for them to see the cover. The title was *Circuitry.*

Alex had no clue what circuitry was.

"It's scintillating," said Luke with a grin.

Scintillating. He had such a huge vocabulary! And obviously he loved circuitry, whatever that was. Alex made a mental note to study up on the subject.

"Well, congrats again, Al. See you soon."

And he and his friends ambled off.

Alex set the coffee down on the table and then fell into her chair. She stared at Emily. "That was Ava's tutor," she said.

"I figured," said Emily. "Wow, he is just the cutest thing ever. And he gave you his coffee!"

Alex stared down at the coffee drink. "He did, didn't he?" she mused. "And he called me Al."

"Sounds like he has a thing for you,"

teased Emily. "Maybe you should ask him to Homecoming."

"Oh, yeah, right," scoffed Alex. "By the way, when *is* Homecoming?"

"In a few weeks," said Emily. "And I'm waiting for Greg Fowler to work up his nerve and ask me to go with him. That boy is *so* shy."

"Does everyone at Ashland Middle School go with a date?" asked Alex. She still felt like a newcomer to the school. She'd moved here to Ashland, Texas, from Boston with her family this past July.

"No, most people just go with friends and stuff," said Emily. "Although Corey and Lindsey will be going as a couple, for sure."

As if Alex needed to be told that! She'd had a tiny crush on Corey O'Sullivan, Lindsey's boyfriend, a while ago, but she was *definitely* over that. "How do their parents feel about their getting back together?" asked Alex. Lindsey's and Corey's parents had gone into the restaurant business together and had had a falling-out last year.

"I think they're fine now," said Emily. "They seem to have reached a shaky truce. And business at Lindsey's family's restaurant has picked up ever since the health department cited the chain across the street from them for health code violations. Hey. You listening?" Emily waved a hand in front of Alex's face.

Alex snapped back to attention. "Sorry," she said. "I was just thinking about Luke. It was really nice of him to give me his coffee. He could have returned it and gotten another one." She took a sip of the coffee and wrinkled her nose.

"Well, he definitely seems to like you," said Emily, taking a noisy last slurp of her smoothie.

"Oh, no, he's just nice like that to everyone," said Alex casually. But inside, her hopes soared. Did Emily mean he seemed to *like* like her? Could he possibly be interested in her? Sure he was in high school, but he was a sophomore. That was only three grades higher than hers.

"Come on, let's go to Cooper and Hunt and try on makeup!" said Emily, standing up and collecting their stuff to throw away. "After all, you're going to be on television!"

In the excitement of running into Luke, Alex had temporarily forgotten about that. Winning the contest and having a high school boy possibly harbor a secret crush on her—this was definitely the best day ever!

CHAPTER TWO

Ava stared at Alex across the dinner table. They weren't supposed to use their phones during mealtimes, but the rules seemed to have slackened with the news that Alex had won the young reporter contest. Of course Ava was happy for Alex, but she could already tell her twin sister was going to be difficult to live with for the next week.

"Sorry, this looks like an important phone call from my production team," said Alex, standing up from the table. "I need to jump on this. Save me some dishes."

Ava glowered at her retreating figure as her sister hurried from the kitchen. "She's starting to throw around showbiz terms a little too much," she pointed out to her parents. "And it's only been a few hours since she found out she won."

"Yes," agreed Mrs. Sackett. "I think we may have to be patient with her, though. It really is a wonderful honor."

Coach smiled wryly. "It's only for a week," he said. "Let her have her moment of glory, Ava. After all, you've certainly had your time in the limelight. You've been the most famous middle schooler in Ashland this year."

Coach was referring to the fact that Ava was the first-ever girl to play for the Ashland Middle School football team. She'd gotten a ton of media attention because of it, even though she hated the spotlight.

"It's not my fault people have nothing better to do than make a big deal of me playing football," grumbled Ava.

Coach patted her arm as he pushed his chair back and stood up. Their Australian shepherd, Moxy, who had been lying contentedly under the table, scrambled to her feet and looked up at him expectantly, as though wondering if an extra walk might be in her future. "Sorry I have to miss our movie night," he said. He stepped around

Moxy and carried the salad bowl to the sink. "I better get going; I'm already running late."

Mrs. Sackett sighed but didn't protest. Ava realized her parents must have discussed this already. What was going on? Sunday nights had been movie nights in the Sackett house for as long as Ava could remember. And now suddenly Alex was on the phone, their older brother, Tommy, was at jazz rehearsal, and Coach was *leaving*? This was the second Sunday in a row he'd missed!

"Where are you going, Coach?" asked Ava, jumping up to help clear the table. "It's my night to choose the movie, and I picked an oldie just for you and Mom!"

"You mean from the 1980s?" he asked as he scraped the leftover chili into a container.

Ava shrugged. "Well, no, the nineties."

"Sorry, sport," he said, patting her curls. "I have to oversee study hall at school again. We have several players on academic probation, so we've set up a supervised study session. It looks like it may be a regular thing for the rest of the season."

"But didn't you do that *last* Sunday too? I thought all the coaches take turns."

Ava noticed Coach and her mom exchange a quick look. Coach didn't say anything, so Ava did.

"Did Coach Byron mess up again?" she asked worriedly.

He hesitated. "His babysitter canceled on him," he said. "It's tough being a single parent, no question. He's struggling with all his personal obligations."

"But it's taking its toll on *our* house too, Michael," said Mrs. Sackett quietly. "First Tommy skips out for his rehearsal, and now you have to go cover for Byron. Yet again."

Coach engulfed her in a bear hug. "I know, hon," he said. "I'll talk to Byron."

Moxy watched him leave and then sank back down onto the floor and heaved a heavy sigh.

Ava moved uneasily around the table, gathering up the napkins. She didn't like the ominous tone in her father's voice. Coach Byron was her favorite of her father's assistant coaches. His kids, Jamila and Shane, were really cute. And it hadn't been very long since his wife had passed away. He was still sad about it, you could tell. What if his job was in trouble just because he couldn't find babysitters?

"I can babysit for him tonight," she said

quickly. "Movie night is no big deal."

"You have your math homework to finish too, sweetie," said Mrs. Sackett. "And I'm still counting on watching the movie with you and Alex after that."

Alex bustled back into the kitchen, her eyes bright. "That was Marcy Maxon's assistant again," she said. "Her name is Candace. Isn't that a cool name?"

"Awesome," said Ava, but of course, Alex didn't pick up on the sarcasm in her tone. Ava didn't look at Mrs. Sackett, but she could feel her mother's disapproving stare.

"Candace was following up on the e-mail she sent me today," Alex continued. "And she told me how great my essay was, and how impressed Marcy Maxon was by it, and she told me Ms. Maxon wants some ideas for my story by Tuesday. I'm supposed to e-mail Ms. Maxon directly!"

"That's wonderful, honey," said Mrs. Sackett.

"So, I'm really sorry, but I just don't think I can participate in our Sunday movie night this week. I need to concept some ideas."

"Did you just use 'concept' as a verb?" asked Ava.

"That's journalism talk," Alex explained. "Anyway, sorry again about missing the movie. Such is the life of a features reporter."

Ava waited for Alex to leave the room before she rolled her eyes. She had expected their mom to object to Alex skipping their movie. Sunday night movies were a time-honored tradition in the Sackett household. Ava knew Alex's story was a big deal, but she wished it didn't have to interfere. She and Mrs. Sackett finished up the dishes together.

Ava underhanded the sponge toward the counter and watched it bounce and then land almost right where it belonged next to the sink. "You do realize that she is going to be impossible to live with," she said to her mother.

Mrs. Sackett smiled. "Let's be happy for her, Ave," she said. "It's a tremendous accomplishment."

"I know. I am happy for her. But a tiny part of me is wondering if the fact that she's Coach's daughter might have had something to do with her winning the contest."

Ava could tell by the look on her mom's face that a similar thought had occurred to her, too. But her mom shrugged. "Everyone can use an angle," she said. "She wouldn't have won if her essay hadn't been terrific. Come on. Go finish up your math, and then let's you and I watch the movie."

The next day at school Ava got to the lunch-room late. She'd forgotten to hand in her science homework and had had to run back to her class-room to put it into the basket. When she walked into the cafeteria, Alex and a big group of their friends were already sitting at a large table, chattering and eating. Ava's friend Kylie moved over to make room for her.

"So how awesome is your twin sister?" Jack Valdeavano said to Ava from across the table.

"She's pretty awesome," said Ava, and mostly meant it.

"We were just talking about what story she should do," said Jack.

Ava appreciated how he made the effort to bring her into the conversation. Jack was great. She still hadn't decided if she liked him "that way," but she always had a lot of fun hanging out with him.

"Alex Sackett, girl reporter," said Corey with a grin.

Lindsey, who was sitting next to Corey, smiled at Alex and helped herself to one of Corey's fries.

Ever since they'd officially started going out again, Lindsey seemed to have adopted a possessive streak with Corey, Ava noted. She always seemed to be wearing his sweatshirt or helping herself to his lunch.

"Do you know what your story's going to be about, Alex?" asked Annelise.

Alex shook her head and stirred her yogurt thoughtfully. "Not yet," she said. "It feels like such a momentous decision. I'm weighing all my options. That's an important first step in the story process."

"So, you guys pumped for Briar Ridge this Saturday?" asked Jack.

Ava was grateful he'd changed the subject before Alex began throwing around too much more of her showbiz talk. "It's always a close game, right, Corey?" she asked. Corey was the quarterback for the Ashland Middle School Tiger Cubs.

Corey nodded. "Every year it seems to be

a really tight contest," he said. "I remember it was even when my older brother was playing. The game doesn't count in the league standings, because Briar Ridge is a private school. But still. We care about beating them."

"Wasn't last year's game controversial?" asked Kylie.

Ava grinned. Kylie had never cared about football before, but now that she and Ava had become friends, Kylie had become a loyal fan of the high school team. She even went to the middle school games now, although Ava suspected it wasn't just to support her: The guy Kylie liked, Owen Rooney, was the wide receiver.

"It was totally controversial," said Jack. Jack played soccer and basketball, not football, but he was good friends with most of the guys on the football team. "Corey completed a touchdown pass to Bobby Evans with two seconds left on the clock, but the officials ruled it incomplete. But the film later showed that both of Bobby's feet were on the ground and in play. You guys got robbed."

"Yeah, well, we'll get revenge for that on Saturday," said Corey. "Especially with our new stud kicker." He grinned at Ava.

"I don't know what's a bigger deal," said Emily. "The Cubs-Colts matchup or Homecoming!"

"They're both going to be so fun!" said Lindsey. She looked at Corey and giggled.

That afternoon when practice was over, Coach Kenerson pulled Ava aside to talk with him. He beckoned her away from the other players, and they went to stand near the fence.

"Did I do something wrong, Coach?" asked Ava anxiously.

"What? Yes. I mean, no," he said, his voice gruffer than usual. "You didn't do anything wrong, Sackett. In fact, you've been doing a good job out there. I like your instincts, your speed, your quickness. With some work you could be a fine receiver."

Ava nodded and waited. He clearly had something on his mind, but it was hard to read his expression behind his mirrored sunglasses. She watched him take off his sunglasses, polish them on his shirt, put them back on, and take them off again. Then he coughed twice. Finally he looked at her.

"I got a call from the Briar Ridge athletic director," he said.

Ava's heart sank. Suddenly she thought she knew what was coming.

"And it seems that, ah, well, it seems that some of the parents there are objecting to, ah, well . . ." He put his sunglasses back on and looked away.

". . . to a girl playing," Ava finished for him quietly.

"Yes. Yes, that's right. To a girl playing."

Ava bumped her helmet against her thigh and scuffed her shoe against the dusty ground. *Here we go again,* she thought.

"As you know," said Coach K, "Briar Ridge is an affluent school, and there are a lot of parents who are lawyers, and a few of them have raised concerns about liability, in the unlikely event that their kid should, ah, cause you to sustain an injury."

"They're worried I'm going to *sue* them?" asked Ava.

Coach took his glasses off again and coughed. "Well, yes, to put it bluntly. But there's the added factor that you're a high-profile kid, Sackett, considering who your father is. I've told the Briar

Ridge AD that I'm going to support you, and so will the Ashland Middle School administration. I told him that if the Colts choose to forfeit the game, they can. They're a private school, so they're not subject to our league rules. He said he'd go back and talk to the parents and the head of school. It's not a final decision. They're still debating. But I wanted to give you a heads-up that this could blow up to be a big issue." He took a deep breath and looked right at Ava. "I'm sorry, Sackett. I know this isn't your doing. I wanted to tell you first, should it actually come to pass. And before I talked to the team."

Ava closed her eyes and groaned softly. "They've been looking forward to this game all year! And now it won't be played because of me."

"*Might* not," he corrected her. "And no matter what happens, let me emphasize that you are in no way responsible for the way this has turned out. It was Briar Ridge's decision."

"Why do people make such a big deal about this?" she asked. "I wish they'd just let me play."

"Me too, Sackett. Me too."

CHAPTER THREE

Alex knocked quietly on Tommy's door, which was partly open. He sat at his desk, noodling around on his electronic keyboard.

"That sounds nice," said Alex, stepping into the room. She frowned at his unmade bed and the heap of clothes on the floor. Moxy lay sprawled on top of a small pile of socks near Tommy's feet. Moxy loved listening to him play and usually nosed her way into his room when he was practicing.

"It's a new piece I'm working on," said Tommy, without pausing his playing. "We've got our first real gig coming up next Saturday night. Downtown, at the Press."

"Ooh, I love that place!" said Alex.

"Have you ever been there?" he asked her dubiously.

"Well, no, not exactly," she admitted, pulling at Tommy's sheets. "But I *hear* it's really great." She made a mental note to check out the Press soon. She knew that it was a combination coffee bar and bookstore, frequented by the cool, smart high school kids and twentysomethings. She'd seen postings around town about shows there—they had poetry readings, and open mike comedy evenings, and performances from local musicians. And now that she was practically in high school and might have a high school boy interested in her, she had to get up to speed about popular high school hangouts.

"Um, what are you doing, Al?" asked Tommy, looking over at her in amusement.

"Making your bed so I can sit down on it," she said. She finished tugging his sheets back into place and smoothing the coverlet. Then she plopped down on the bed and sat cross-legged, her chin in her hands. She didn't often spend one-on-one time with Tommy, or at least, not as often as Ava did. They seemed to have a special bond, those two. But with her ever-growing crush on Luke, she realized that having a high schooler for an older brother was an untapped resource. *And* Tom and Luke were friends! She needed to take advantage of this opportunity.

He finished his song, a jazzy, bluesy tune over a walking bass line, and then set the keyboard aside and pulled out his math book.

"The Press is such a cool place! It's so . . . European," said Alex, trying to keep Tommy's focus away from his math homework, at least for another few minutes.

"Yeah, we were psyched to be asked to perform there. We're not getting paid for it, but it's great exposure." He pulled out his calculator and a pad of graph paper.

"So can I ask you something?" asked Alex.

Tommy set down his calculator and half turned toward her. "Yes?" he asked when she hesitated.

"Um, how does a guy act when—I mean, how can a girl tell if a guy likes her?"

Tommy gave her a sly look. "Just wondering, are you?"

She felt herself flush. "Just answer, please?"

"Welllll," Tommy considered, pressing all ten of his fingertips together lightly, "it's usually not too hard to tell. Guys aren't all that subtle."

"Well, see, there is this guy-who-will-remain-nameless," said Alex, suddenly breathless, "and I think he might like me, I mean, you know, *like* like me"—her words came out in a gush—"because, for instance, he hugged me, and—"

"He *hugged* you? Whoa!" said Tommy in mock surprise, waggling his palms and leaning backward in his chair.

"I *know*, and he seems to like to talk to me, about books and stuff, and the way he seems to avoid looking at me sometimes, makes me think he's really shy, and then the other day he bought me this really fancy pumpkin-spiced coffee drink from the pricey coffee place in the mall." She took a breath, pausing to consider whether it was technically accurate to say he'd bought it for her. "Well, we kind of shared it," she amended.

"I see," said Tommy, nodding his head wisely. "I would say that the fact that he bought you a fancy coffee is probably a sign that he's interested. Guys your age don't usually have a reliable source of income, so if he shelled out big bucks for a pumpkin-spice latte, you're probably right about how he feels about you."

"You think so?" asked Alex, clasping her hands together. She didn't correct his assumption that her crush was her age. What difference did a few years make?

"Yeah, sounds like it. Is he super nerdy like you?"

"Yes!" said Alex without bothering to take offense at this. "He seems to read all the time. Practically every time I've seen him, he has a book with him."

"Okay, so you two can talk books then," said Tommy. "And speaking of books, I need to get my math done before I head out to rehearsal, so you better head out now, okay, champ?"

"Wait! Do you think I should ask him to Homecoming, or wait for him to ask me?"

"Maybe he's already planning to, but he's waiting to do it the right way," said Tommy. "For our Homecoming, there's a big contest for the 'cute ask,' where the person who thinks of the most clever way to ask someone gets in free and wins some prize."

Alex considered this. Maybe Luke was planning a big surprise for her.

"Now am-scray, okay?" said Tommy. "I have to get this done."

"One last thing," said Alex. "Do you have any ideas for what my story can be about? My news story, that is? My producer, Marcy Maxon, has told me that I need an idea by end of the day tomorrow. I want it to be really different, really unique."

"Al, I am sure you'll think of something great," said Tommy. "You inherited more than your share of Sackett brainpower. So go think about it. And vamoose, squirt. Some of us have to actually work to get our mediocre grades."

Alex jumped off the bed, scampered to her room, and opened her computer. She tried to concentrate on coming up with story ideas for her piece, but her thoughts kept drifting to Luke. She needed to come up with interesting, high-school-level topics to discuss with him next time he came over. Hadn't he been carrying a book on circuitry when she ran into him at the mall? She clicked into the online catalog for her school's library. A book on circuitry. That's what she'd read, so she could casually work that topic into a conversation the next time he came over to tutor Ava.

She scrolled through the titles: *Circuit Analysis Decoded. The Circuit Designer's Guide.*

Foundations of Digital Circuits. "Yikes," she muttered. "Not exactly beach reading."

"What are you working on?" asked Ava from the doorway.

Alex jumped, and quickly minimized her computer screen. "Oh, just thinking up some story ideas," she said.

Ava gave her a look that needed no explanation. The twins often sensed what the other was really feeling or thinking, and Ava could always see through Alex when she was faking something.

Alex sighed and smiled guiltily. "Well, to tell you the truth, I was also semi-obsessing about a guy I have a crush on," she admitted. "I was just looking something up about him."

Ava's eyes narrowed. "Is it Corey?"

"Corey? No, *definitely* not Corey," said Alex quickly. "He and Lindsey are totally back together, and I'm completely over him. I mean, he's great, and nice and obviously extremely cute, but we're just friends. No, this is someone else, but I'm not ready to divulge his name to you, because I'm still not positive he likes me." She suppressed a little grin. "Although I think he does."

"So then why so secretive?" asked Ava. "You know I'd never tell anyone anything."

"Just . . . because," said Alex. She didn't want to tell Ava that she had a crush on her tutor, who happened also to be in high school. Sometimes Ava had a tendency to see the downside of things, and Alex wanted to enjoy this giddy feeling of having a crush on someone before Ava could burst her bubble.

Ava frowned, shrugged, and turned to leave.

"Wait! Ave?"

Ava came back to Alex's doorway.

"Is anything wrong? You look a little, I don't know, upset?"

Ava shook her head quickly. "We had a tough practice today," she said. "And—well, I'm not ready to divulge anything to you right this very moment."

"Oh," said Alex, feeling a little hurt. But then again, she'd just said the exact same thing to Ava.

Ava turned and left.

Alex stared at the place where her sister had been standing. This didn't feel right. She and Ava never kept secrets from each other. Maybe she should have told her about Luke after all.

CHAPTER FOUR

On Tuesday after practice, Coach Kenerson gathered the team together and told them to take a knee. Ava felt her stomach coil up like a tightly wound spring. She knew what was coming.

"I talked to the Briar Ridge athletic director," said Coach K, vigorously polishing his sunglasses. "And I'm afraid I have some disappointing news."

A murmur rippled through the crowd of players.

"Briar Ridge has, ah . . . Briar Ridge will not be playing us on Saturday."

A loud cry of protest erupted.

Coach K raised his hands to quiet them. "I know. It's disappointing. It seems that the Briar

Ridge administration has chosen to listen to a small but very vocal minority of parents who are concerned about playing us."

"Why?" demanded Xander Browning. "Are they afraid we'll wallop them?" He rammed his ham-size fist into his palm menacingly.

"No, no, it's not that. It's, ah, about, ah, playing against a team with, ah . . ." Coach K stopped and looked to the right and to the left, but his assistant coaches suddenly became fascinated by their own shoes.

Ava felt everyone's eyes on her. Her face burned. She wanted to put her helmet back on, but that would be too obvious. She, too, stared at the ground. An ant was crawling across her cleat, and she concentrated on its wobbly route between her laces.

Coach K didn't have to finish his sentence. Everyone knew why Briar Ridge had chosen to forfeit the game.

Corey was the first to respond. "Okay, fine," he said. "We'll take the win, and they'll forfeit. Not our problem."

"It stinks that we don't get to play them," said Kal Tippett. "I was really looking forward to getting revenge for last year's game. Now they'll be able to keep bragging about how they beat us for a whole 'nother year."

There were murmurs of agreement.

"Hey! What if Sackett sits it out?" asked Andy Baker. "Would they play us then?"

Ava held her breath. Leave it to Andy Baker to be the one to ask that question. Ashland Middle School wouldn't ever let Briar Ridge get away with such a thing . . . right? If *they* got away with it, what would stop every other opponent they played from saying the same thing?

"She's not going to sit out!" said Corey hotly. "We need her. She's our best kicker and you know it, Baker. Especially now that Xander's my blocker. Besides, why should we give them what they want when they're acting so stupid?"

Ava's heart swelled with gratitude toward Corey.

Andy scowled. Some of his friends were talking in low voices, saying stuff Ava couldn't hear. But she knew they thought she ought to volunteer to sit out the game.

"Sackett's not sitting out. That's not going to happen, Baker," Coach K chimed in. "Our administration is behind us the whole way. We play with Sackett, or we don't play. That's final."

Ava stared harder at the ground. Now the ant was crawling toward her helmet, which was on the ground next to her. It must look like the Superdome to the ant. What if Andy was right? It did seem dumb to make her whole team lose out on the opportunity to play a game they'd been looking forward to for so long. But her whole life she'd been taught to stand up for herself. She wished her dad were here to talk this over with her. She decided to stay quiet.

No one said anything to her as they walked toward the locker rooms. The whole team was somber, their disappointment palpable.

Practice had run late, so Ava had the girls' locker room all to herself. She'd miss the late bus if she didn't hustle, but she didn't care. She'd walk. She didn't feel like seeing or talking to anyone right now.

Dinner wasn't quite ready, so Alex checked her e-mail for the fifth time in five minutes. She'd sent Marcy Maxon her story ideas and was waiting to hear what her response would be. She'd been nervous to send the e-mail—Emily was right, Marcy Maxon *was* somewhat of a celebrity in Ashland. She was supersmart and super stylish, with blond hair and perfect skin, and a big, Broadway-style voice that was tinged with a Texas accent.

Finally her laptop dinged. She had a message from Marcy!

These ideas are not working for me, Alexandra. A feature about a day in the life of a seventh-grade class president doesn't have the heartstring appeal I'm looking for. And your community service organizing to fund the new scoreboard is on the right track, but it's already happened. We would have nothing to work with visually.

Give me a good human-interest story. Focus on the Sackett family. That will attract a wide viewership. Yours is a high-profile last name. Don't you have a sister who plays football? Work that angle. Remember: A good reporter has to make sacrifices, Alexandra.

The first sentence stung. Television people could be so abrupt! What did Marcy Maxon even mean? Alex had been so sure one of her ideas would appeal to her, but it seemed like nothing did. And a story about Ava? Been there, done that. Yes, it was cool that Ava was the first-ever girl to play for the AMS team, but the media frenzy was over. Now she was just a player like everyone else. There was no controversy anymore. Everyone had accepted that a girl was on the team. Alex sighed. She was never going to think of something.

By the time Ava got home, dinner was on the table. Tommy, Alex, and Mrs. Sackett had already started eating. Ava stepped over Moxy, washed her hands at the sink, and slid into her seat. "Sorry I'm late," she mumbled. "Where's Coach?"

Mrs. Sackett grimaced. "He said he'd be home late again," she said. "That's the life of a big-time Texas football coach."

Ava's heart sank. She had hoped to be able to talk to her dad about her football situation. He always seemed to make her feel better, no matter what the problem was.

"Saw him in a powwow with Coach Byron and the others on my way out," said Tommy, pouring himself another huge glass of milk.

That only made Ava feel more anxious. Was

Coach Byron going to get fired? Surely her dad wouldn't let that happen. But then again, there were forces in the Ashland football program that were beyond her dad's control.

Alex barely touched her food and seemed lost in thought, drumming her fingers on the table.

"Al's bumming," said Tommy, plopping a gigantic pile of roasted sweet potatoes onto his plate. "She still needs an idea for a story."

Alex didn't even seem to hear him. She nibbled on her knuckle, her brow furrowed with concentration.

"How was your day, Ave?" asked Mrs. Sackett.

"Not great," said Ava. She took a deep breath, and then told them about the Briar Ridge situation.

Tommy whistled. "That's lame," he said.

"It's outrageous!" said Mrs. Sackett, indignation written across her face. "Just wait until you tell your father about this! The idea!"

"It's awesome!" Alex blurted out. Ava's information appeared to have revived her.

The other three turned to look at Alex.

"*This* will be my big story!" she said. "An exposé about Briar Ridge School's refusal to play football against my twin sister! I'll e-mail Ms. Maxon and pitch this idea to her! Mom, may I please be excused?"

"No, Alex, you may not," said Mrs. Sackett firmly. "It can wait until after dinner."

"And also," said Ava, "don't I get a say in this decision?" This was the last thing in the world she wanted Alex to report about. But just then the kitchen door opened and Coach tramped in, looking weary. Moxy sprang up to greet him, her back end wagging wildly.

He leaned over and kissed Mrs. Sackett on the top of her head, then headed to the sink to scrub his hands.

"Sorry, honey," he said, toweling off.

Mrs. Sackett was already heaping his plate with chicken and potatoes. "Byron again?" she asked in a low voice.

Coach nodded. "His kids have a dentist appointment," he said, pouring himself a glass of water. "He has to miss practice tomorrow, so we were going over the practice plan with the other coaches. Anyway, how were everyone's days?"

"Ava has something to tell you about football," said Mrs. Sackett.

"What's up, sweet pea?" he asked Ava.

Ava frowned. Her father seemed preoccupied, like he was only half listening. But she told him about Briar Ridge. "So part of me feels like I should just sit it out so my team can play, but Mom is outraged by that idea and wants me to stand up for myself."

Instead of reacting with indignation, Coach just nodded. He took a thoughtful sip of water and set his glass down carefully. "Whatever you decide, I'm sure it'll be for the good of the team, Ave," he said.

That's a perplexing statement, thought Ava. She'd expected him to agree with her mom and encourage her to take a stand. Instead he seemed like he had barely registered what she'd said.

"And whatever you decide, Ave, I just want you to know that it's brilliant for me," said Alex excitedly. "I finally have a perfect news story for Ms. Maxon. I can't wait to tell her! I mean, I can't wait to pitch it to her. That's how you suggest an idea for a story: You pitch it. She's been making suggestions that my story be focused on my family, and being a Sackett and stuff, because everyone knows who Daddy is. She'll be so psyched!"

Ava rose from the table. "But I don't want

you to do a story about me," she said to Alex in a firm, strong voice.

Alex froze. "Wait, what?"

"I'm sick of being the center of attention in these dumb news stories. I need your support here, Al, and I don't want you joining the other side. So, no. You have to think of something else." A few too many times, Ava had found herself in situations she didn't like, just because she had a hard time saying no to her sister. Her mind flashed back to events of a few weeks before, when Alex had talked her into switching places so that Ava could try out for cheerleading, pretending to be Alex. There had been disastrous consequences. Well, not this time. This time, she would stand her ground.

The rest of her family had gone quiet. Tommy even stopped eating for a moment. They all seemed surprised by Ava's sudden firmness, but Ava didn't care.

Mrs. Sackett spoke first. "Alex, you need to respect your sister's decision," she said. "And anyway, since there's not going to be a game on Saturday, you won't have much to report about, right? I'm sure you'll think of something else."

"Your mother's right, Alex," said Coach. "Your

sister has a right to her privacy."

Alex shrugged. "Okay, okay, fine," she said. "If that's the way you feel about it, Ave."

Alex sounded wounded, but Ava tried not to let it bother her. "Yes. That's the way I feel about it." She left the kitchen without even asking if she could be excused from the table.

CHAPTER FIVE

Alex sank into her desk chair, lost in thought. Ava was upset, and Alex understood why—she knew how much her twin hated to be in the spotlight. But this story was bigger than Ava. It was about women's rights, and fighting injustice. And Ms. Maxon had told her that for a good reporter, getting the story was everything. If you had to upset some people in order to get it, well, so be it. She would still do the story, even if it meant upsetting Ava. Hadn't Ms. Maxon written that a good reporter had to make sacrifices? Now Alex understood what that meant. And besides, once Ava saw the piece, she'd see why Alex was right. She'd understand. There was the small matter of what to shoot that she needed to think about. With no game being played, she'd need to be creative about how to do the story. If Ava wasn't willing to be interviewed, then maybe she could get Coach Kenerson, and Corey, and some of Ava's teammates to talk. And maybe she could surprise the athletic director of Briar Ridge School with a camera on his way into work one morning, catch him off guard, the way some of those hard-hitting news programs did.

Alex turned to her computer and typed up the idea, her fingers flying with excitement. Then she sent it off to Marcy Maxon.

Later that evening, Luke came over for a tutoring session with Ava.

"Why don't you two work in the study tonight, rather than at the kitchen table?" suggested Mrs. Sackett, after Luke had finished greeting Moxy, who'd gone wild with delight upon seeing him again. "That way you won't be constantly interrupted."

Ava thought that was a good suggestion, considering how frequently Alex had found reasons to traipse through the kitchen the last few times Luke had been there.

"Okay, so how's pre-algebra going?" asked Luke, as soon as they were settled next to each other at the desk in the study, and Moxy had shimmied her way under the desk at their feet.

"So-so, I guess," said Ava. She curled her bare toes into Moxy's fur. Moxy heaved a contented sigh. "During class, I get bogged down taking notes. By the time I finish writing down what the teacher said, she's moved on to the next thing, and—"

There was a hesitant knock at the door, and Alex walked in.

"Sorry to interrupt you, Ava," she said. "Oh! Hi!" She acted surprised to see Luke.

Yeah, right. Ava knew that Alex had known full well Luke was coming tonight.

"By the way, Ave, have you seen my library book?"

Ava's eyes narrowed. Alex had changed out of the comfy flannel pants and T-shirt that she'd been wearing at dinner, and now wore her new blue shirt and formfitting jeans. Ava could also see that she had sparkly pink lip gloss on. "No, Alex," she sighed. "I haven't seen your book."

"Oh! There it is!" said Alex brightly, and strode to the side table next to the couch. "Thought I'd left it in here. Oh, whoops!"

The book seemed to jump out of her hands. It landed on the floor next to Luke, who stooped to retrieve it for her.

"*Circuitry Fun*, huh?" he said, reading the title as he handed it over. "Little light reading?"

"Since when do you read books about circuitry?" asked Ava.

"Oh, I just thought it looked interesting," said Alex with a little laugh. She turned to Luke. "I'll bet you know all about circuitry," she said. "Have you formulated a simplified way to evaluate high-speed switching circuits?"

Luke blinked at her. "I have no clue what you're talking about."

Alex tried to laugh it off, but Ava could see she was mortified.

"Funny coincidence, though," Luke continued. "Because just the other day I had to slog through a chapter on circuitry for my physics homework. It's tough going if you're not into that sort of thing. I'm more of an English and history guy, I admit." He bopped Ava playfully over the head with his pencil. "Although

I think I can handle helping this one with her pre-algebra."

He turned back to the book, and out of the corner of her eye Ava watched Alex trudge dejectedly out of the room.

It couldn't be. Could it? Ava thought. Was it possible that Luke was the guy Alex thought had a crush on her? It was obvious from a million miles away that Alex had a major crush on him, but where in the world did she get the idea that it was reciprocal? He was nice to her, of course, but he was nice to everyone. Surely Alex couldn't be that dense. Ava shook her head, planted her elbow on the desk, and sank her chin into the palm of her hand. *Not again with the Alex drama,* she thought, and then turned to focus on what Luke was saying.

Upstairs in her room, Alex threw herself back onto her bed and sighed dramatically. She was so envious of the easy way Ava and Luke had. What was the vocab word she'd just learned? *Rapport.* That was it. Spelled with a *t* at the end, but you didn't pronounce it. She was so envious of the easy *rapport* they had. Although it was certainly a relief not to have to read any more about circuitry. She sat up and tossed the book onto her desk, and then fell backward onto her bed again, conjuring an image of Luke's curly, sandy-colored hair. Those baby-blanket-blue eyes. She replayed the scene from moments before. Hadn't he dropped his gaze after their eyes had met? He'd smiled so warmly—showing that extremely adorable dimple in his right cheek. What if he really were secretly pining for her? Their whole relationship felt so *Romeo and Juliet*—the forbidden love between them. And so what if he was in high school and she was in middle school? They weren't *that* far apart in age. Why, her own parents were a few years apart!

Her e-mail plinked, and she sat up to see who the sender was. Marcy Maxon!

You're on the right track, Alexandra. A Sackett family story would have real crossover appeal for our viewers. But if it's a forfeit, there's no story. So you need to talk your sister into agreeing to sit out. THEN we'll have a story. She agrees not to play, we film the big game showing her sitting on the sidelines, and then we do an exclusive interview with her. Get your father there too.

So let me know after you've spoken with your sister, and I'll arrange for the crew to meet you at the game on Saturday.

Alex gulped. This was a new wrinkle. How was she supposed to talk Ava into agreeing not to play, let alone convince her to let herself be filmed? Sitting out would go against everything their parents had taught them about standing up for yourself. And even if Ava did opt out, there was no guarantee Coach Kenerson would accept her decision. Alex groaned. What a complicated mess.

A text came in from Emily.

Greg Fowler still hasn't asked me to Homecoming. If he doesn't, should we just plan to go together, you and me?

Alex replied:

He will ask you. Don't worry.

That would be very awkward if Alex told Emily she'd go with her to Homecoming and then Luke finally worked up the nerve to ask her. Homecoming was coming up quickly. She had to show him more signs of encouragement, send him messages that yes, it was okay to ask her and yes, she would say yes if he did.

Will we go to the high school dance, or the middle school dance? she wondered.

The idea of going to the high school dance excited her, but then she wouldn't get to hang out with all her friends—or show off her adorable date!

It doesn't matter, she decided. *Either way I'll get to go with Luke.*

Her thoughts were interrupted by a knock at the door.

"Honey?" Mrs. Sackett said, stepping over to Alex's desk. "May I ask that you not interrupt Luke and Ava while they're working together? You know your sister has a hard enough time concentrating. I thought putting them in the study would be a good plan, but we all need to let them work in peace."

"Yes, sure, Mom," said Alex, trying to keep her tone neutral. "Sorry about that."

Mrs. Sackett nodded appreciatively and left.

Just like Romeo and Juliet, Alex thought. Their *families tried to keep* them *apart too. But true love will prevail.*

CHAPTER SIX

"Okay, Bryce, that was better," said Ava. She trotted back to Bryce Hobson, a skinny sixth grader who also played kicker, and dumped the four footballs she'd retrieved onto the ground in front of him. "Now this time, make sure to keep your head down and kick through the ball," she said. "And don't forget to keep your shoulders and hips in line with the center of the goalpost."

Bryce blew out a puff of air and picked up one of the footballs. "It's hard to get fired up when I know we don't even have a game this Saturday," he grumbled. Then he looked at her guiltily, as though it had just dawned on him that she was the reason they weren't playing. "No offense," he added.

Ava pretended not to be bothered. "Yeah, I know it's hard to keep the energy up, but Coach wants us to go hard in practice like it's a game situation," she said. But she knew he was right. She could sense a general feeling of "why bother?" from her teammates, and she didn't blame them. Without the Briar Ridge game to look forward to, it was tough to feel enthusiastic and to give it their all in practice. They'd worked so hard, all season, and Briar Ridge was one of their biggest opponents. For the zillionth time, she felt guilty, knowing she had the power to change the situation. All she had to do was to say she would sit out, and the game could go on.

But wasn't that giving in? Wasn't that letting them get away with it? She thought back to what Coach had said the night before. "Whatever you decide, I'm sure it will be for the good of the team." Why was she the one who had to decide? It didn't seem fair.

When practice was over, Coach K called the team together for a talk. For a fleeting moment Ava's hopes soared, thinking that maybe Briar Ridge had backed down and she'd be allowed to play with her team. But one look at Coach K's grim face told her the Briar Ridge parents hadn't changed their minds.

"The situation with Briar Ridge has not changed, unfortunately," he said.

A loud groan arose from the boys. Ava stared at the ground. Where was that little ant when she needed it?

"Isn't there *anything* we can do, Coach?" asked Andy Baker.

Ava didn't look up, but she felt him look her way and was well aware of the emphasis he'd placed on the word "anything."

Corey spoke up. "Listen, guys, we play with Sackett or we don't play," he said. "She's our best kicker. She's our *only*—" He stopped. "She's an important part of the team," he corrected himself.

Ava knew he had been about to say *our only kicker* but must have realized he would hurt Bryce's feelings. Bryce wasn't terrible, but he was still so young, and still learning the technique. Plus, being a kicker meant you had to be able to deal with high-stress, high-pressure situations. Bryce was untested, and she was pretty sure Corey didn't trust him to be calm under difficult conditions. And Xander was a punter, which was a completely different kind of kicking, and he had more or less decided he wanted to play defense.

The other boys mostly nodded in agreement with Corey, but Andy and some of his buddies didn't look happy.

"Guys, the decision is yours, and I'll stick by it," said Coach K. "I like your team spirit. It's a credit to AMS and to your character."

Which only made Ava feel worse than ever.

By lunchtime on Thursday everyone at school had heard Briar Ridge was forfeiting, and everyone knew why. Ava was once again aware that she was the center of attention, the last place she wanted to be. As she wound her way through the tables toward where Alex and their friends were sitting, she sensed that kids stopped talking as she passed them. Her face was burning by the time she slid in between Kylie and Lindsey. Alex was across from her.

"We are so bummed!" said Lindsey before Ava had even taken a bite of her peanut butter and

jelly sandwich. "The cheer squad has been working really hard on a new routine for Saturday's
game! I can't believe the Briar Ridge players and
cheerleaders are accepting this ridiculous decision! I mean, hello? Can you say 'twenty-first
century'?"

Ava managed a tight smile, and then took a
glum bite of her sandwich. Coach had forgotten to cut the crusts off this morning, a sign of
how distracted he was these days. He always
cut them off for her. Well, she could hardly com-
plain. She chewed the dry crust and swallowed
it down.

"Are you going to do your news piece about
this?" Kylie asked Alex. "About Ava and football
and Briar Ridge forfeiting the game rather than
playing against a girl?"

Ava looked at Alex sharply. She waited to
hear Alex tell everyone publicly that she wasn't
going to do the story.

"Oh—ha-ha, that's a crazy idea," said Alex.
"Ava hates being the center of controversy. Kylie,
I just love your shirt. Is it new?"

Ava looked at Alex with narrowed eyes. Was
she trying to change the subject? Well, if she
was, maybe that was a good thing. Because Ava

didn't want to talk about the stupid Briar Ridge game either. Knowing her sister, she'd probably thought of five new ideas for her story. Thank goodness Alex had gotten *this* idea out of her mind.

"Well, I think the whole thing with Briar Ridge is completely idiotic," Kylie said. "I just wish they'd let you play, Ava. Someone should start a protest or something."

"I agree," said Corey.

Lindsey nodded. She picked up Corey's baseball cap, which he'd placed on the table between them, and put it on her own head, backward.

"Thanks, you guys," said Ava.

After lunch, Alex hurried to catch up to Ava. They headed to their lockers, which were side by side.

"So have you decided what you're going to do?" asked Alex, as she put her lunch bag away into her neatly organized shelving unit. "I mean, about the game."

Ava looked at her, confused. She was trying to tug her social studies book out of the unsteady pile of books and papers in the top section of her locker without dislodging the whole stack. "I'm not *doing* anything," she said. "It was my teammates' decision not to play without me, so Briar Ridge has chosen to forfeit the game."

Alex nodded. "Yeah, I know. Of course, no one on your team should ever ask you to say you won't play. But I just wondered . . . if you had thought about not playing. Your decision, you know. It could be a statement of its own— you 'taking one for the team,' if you know what I mean." She used air quotes to dramatize her point.

Ava blinked at her. Was Alex suggesting what Ava *thought* she was suggesting? "You think I should cave in to the Briar Ridge people? That I should tell my team to play the game without me?"

"Well, it's just something I thought you *might* consider," said Alex quickly. "I mean, it's not the craziest idea in the world. Think about it: You'd be the hero for your teammates, and they'd probably be spurred on to win the game on your behalf."

Ava slumped against her locker, feeling utterly confused. Her empty lunch bag, which she'd stuffed into a corner of her locker, popped back out and landed on the floor. She wanted this situation to be out of her hands, to have the outcome determined by other people. She was just a kid, a kid who liked to play football. She hated the fact that something she agreed to do or not do would have such a huge impact on everyone concerned. First her dad, and now her own sister, encouraging her to make this into a decision? Her head began to pound. Maybe Alex was right.

Just after the final bell rang that afternoon, Ava hurried to find Coach Kenerson before practice. He was packing up his stuff at his desk.

"Sackett," he said. "What's up?"

Ava took a deep breath. "Coach, I've made a decision," she said. "I'm going to sit out on Saturday. I want my teammates to be able to play that game."

Coach K stopped shuffling through a stack of papers and blinked at her over his half-glasses. He seemed to be struggling to figure out how to react to Ava's decision. Finally he said, "You sure about that, Sackett?"

Ava thought she detected a hint of eagerness in his tone, and immediately she felt better about her decision. Even her coach wanted the game to be played! "I'm sure," she said with more confidence now. "It's not everyone else's fault that the other team is being stupid and refusing to play. Our team shouldn't be punished for that. And I'll work with Bryce today and tomorrow and help him with his kicking. He's improved a lot, even this week."

Coach K came around his desk and extended his large hand out for Ava to shake. She did, awkwardly. His grip was strong.

"I like your sense of team spirit, Sackett," he said. "That shows real character, real class. What Briar Ridge is doing is wrong, and I hate letting them get away with it, but I appreciate you putting the team ahead of all this nonsense."

"Thanks, Coach," said Ava, quietly nursing her throbbing hand behind her back.

"Also," he added with a sly grin, "I'm not going to lie. I'm looking forward to playing on Saturday because I want to kick Briar Ridge's butt."

CHAPTER SEVEN

At dinner that night, Alex was once again preoccupied. What a mess. If Ava would only agree to sit out, she'd have a story. But Ava could be so stubborn, so *principled* sometimes. Alex gloomily rolled a pea back and forth across her plate.

Tommy was chattering away about his concert on Saturday night. "We've just recorded our first EP, and we're going to be selling it at the door."

"What's an EP?" asked Coach.

Tommy rolled his eyes. "The fact that you don't know that, Coach, is precisely why you and Mom are not allowed to be there," he said. "No offense."

"It means an 'extended play' sound track," explained Mrs. Sackett. "He thinks it's embarrassing to have his old, uncool parents there, even though one of us knows what an EP is."

Alex kept rolling the pea around, only half listening.

"You looked it up online," said Tom with a grin. "And you still can't come. Coach tends to attract his own crowd when he goes out into the world, in case you hadn't noticed."

"I understand, darling," said Mrs. Sackett.

"Um, I made a decision," said Ava suddenly.

Something about her tone caused everyone to stop and pay attention to her. Even Alex stopped playing with her food and looked at her.

"I've decided to sit out the game on Saturday."

Coach and Mrs. Sackett both set their forks down and stared at Ava. Tommy's eyebrows shot up in surprise.

Alex couldn't believe what she'd just heard Ava say. It was as though Ava had read her thoughts! The twins had, of course, been doing just that their whole lives—Tommy called it their creepy twin thing. They didn't just finish each other's sentences. They often seemed to sense what the other was thinking before the other had thought it yet. But how amazing was it for Ava to sense how badly Alex wanted to do this story about her, even if Ava didn't realize it herself?

Finally Tommy gave a low whistle. "You sure, Ave?" he asked. "That's kind of an epic decision."

Alex could barely contain her joy, but she carefully set down her fork and composed herself so she wouldn't appear too excited. "I think it's really admirable of you, Ave," she said. Then she added, "If you feel like it's the best decision, I mean."

Mrs. Sackett gave Coach a look, and he seemed to understand that she wanted him to be the one to comment.

He put down his napkin and pushed his plate away, leaning toward Ava. "Honey," he said. "I know this wasn't an easy decision for you. We've raised you to stick to your principles and to try to do what's right, what's just. But this really is a tricky situation, and I respect your decision. Sometimes it feels right to put aside your indignation at the injustice of a situation and do what's best for your team. Your mother and I support your decision."

"So does your twin sister!" said Alex, trying

not to bounce up and down in her chair. She leaped up to clear her plate. "I better get to work on my homework."

As soon as she'd put in her share of cleaning up and putting away food, she hurried to her room to e-mail Marcy Maxon.

Just moments after she'd sent the e-mail, her phone vibrated. Marcy Maxon was calling her!

"Alexandra? Marcy Maxon here."

"Oh! Hi!" said Alex, suddenly breathless.

"Good work talking your sister into the plan. *Now* you have a story. I like it a lot."

Alex breathed a sigh of relief. Marcy Maxon liked it!

". . . and plenty of human interest," Marcy Maxon was saying. "Your sister will look great on camera. We can do an interview with the Briar Ridge coach and AD, real close-up shots with tough questions. Love it. What time is the game on Saturday?"

"It's at ten," replied Alex. "But, ah, Ms. Maxon?"

"This is showbiz, Alexandra. Call me Marcy."

"Um, okay then, um, Marcy," Alex replied, thrilled to the core. "And you can call *me* Alex. Here's the thing I should mention: My sister wasn't that enthusiastic about me doing a story about her. She doesn't like to be the center of media attention the way I do."

"Well then, talk her into it," said Marcy promptly.

"Oh! Ah-ha-ha! I'll try," replied Alex, but it was a hollow laugh. "It's just that—"

"Make it happen, Alexandra," Marcy said.

"Okay," said Alex in a tiny voice. How in the world was she going to get Ava to agree to this story?

"And keep the whole thing quiet," Marcy cut in. "Don't go talking it up around the mall, or wherever middle school kids congregate these days. We want this to be an exclusive. No media circus. We'll come shoot the high school game tomorrow night and do some backstory. We can get some shots of your brother—what's his name? Tim?"

"Tom," said Alex.

"Tom. Yes. He's on your father's team, yes?"

"Yes, but—"

"And your father, of course. Maybe your mother, too. Will she be there?"

"Oh, um, sure."

"Good. That will look good. We can get some footage in the can, maybe you can prep a little intro piece."

"But what if—"

"Then we'll show up at your sister's game on Saturday. What's her name? Anna?"

"Ava."

"Don't even tell Anna that we're coming. That way, we'll be the only crew there filming, and you can control the way the story is told. She'll be fine with it once she sees it."

"Well, maybe, but—"

"So we'll meet you at the high school main gate, twenty minutes before kickoff tomorrow night."

The phone clicked off.

Alex stared at it for a bit longer. *Would* Ava mind? Should she really not even mention that the TV people would be there? *Surely she'll come around once she sees what an awesome piece it will be,* Alex thought.

But a tiny voice deep down told her that Ava really wouldn't be okay with it. Alex tried to ignore it.

And then Luke Grabowski was standing at the doorway to her room. All thoughts of Ava flew from her head.

Alex leaped up quickly, knocking over her chair and nearly falling backward onto it. She recovered her balance, but just barely, and tried to pretend she'd meant to do it.

"Oh! Hey!" she said, casually righting the chair back onto its four legs.

"Hey yourself," said Luke, grinning that one-dimpled smile of his.

Alex's legs went weak. Was this the moment? Was he going to ask her to Homecoming?

"I brought you something," he said.

Flowers? A locket? A charm bracelet? Some other token of his love for her?

But Luke was holding out a book. A very thick book.

"I don't know if you've ever read Dickens," he said, "but he's one of my all-time favorites."

"Ah," said Alex. She took the book he was holding out to her—a well-thumbed paperback called *David Copperfield*. It looked like it was about two thousand pages long. "Thanks," she said, trying hard to keep the disappointment out of her voice.

He shrugged. "I don't know, maybe you're not old enough yet, but—"

"I'm really super mature for my age!" she blurted out, and then immediately regretted saying it. Why did she have to act like such a dork around guys she liked?

"Anyway, you can keep it," he said. "I have two copies. Well, off to see Ave. See ya, Al."

"See ya."

He poked his head back around. "Oh! Forgot to ask you—"

Her heart stopped.

"Are you going to your brother's gig Saturday night?"

Her heart resumed beating. "Um—I—um, yes?" She'd almost forgotten about Tommy's concert at the Press.

"Cool. Should be awesome. I told them I'd sell their EP at the door for them, so I'll see you there."

And he left.

Okay, so he hadn't asked her to Homecoming. But he'd called her Al! And he'd basically asked her out on a date for Saturday night!

She fanned through the pages of the book, searching for a note he might have tucked into it, asking her to Homecoming. Nothing. Of course not. Luke was too classy to ask her by way of a note. He'd do it in person for sure. That's why he'd made plans with her for this Saturday. That was when he was planning to pop the question. Maybe he was planning it as a big surprise.

CHAPTER EIGHT

Friday night's high school game, the Ashland Tigers against the Culver City Cougars, was at home. Ava caught a ride to the stadium with Coach and Tommy, as she usually did. She liked to get there early and stand near the fence behind the bench, where she could watch Coach and Tommy's team warm up. For her, watching warm-ups was almost as exciting as the actual game—the feelings of anticipation, suspense, and teamwork were palpable as the special teams went through their warm-ups and drills. Tommy was a quarterback, but he rarely got into games, as the star quarterback was PJ Kelly. Tommy didn't seem to mind all that much that he rarely played, though. Even though he seemed to be focusing more on football these days to appease Coach as play-offs approached, Ava suspected Tommy's heart was leaning more toward music.

"Hi, Ava!" yelled Shane Hardy, Coach Byron's six-year-old son. He and his four-year-old sister, Jamila, raced over to her. They'd been playing on the bleachers.

Ava gave them each a big hug. She loved little kids, and she'd hit it off with Shane and Jamila right away. "Where's your babysitter?" she asked them, looking around.

"No babysitter tonight!" said Jamila excitedly.

"Daddy says we get to sit with the team during the game!" added Shane, bouncing up and down.

Ava frowned. She remembered what Coach had said to her mom about Coach Byron's frequent absences. She hoped people wouldn't mind if Shane and Jamila were on the bench for the game. She hoped his job wasn't in jeopardy.

"Well, you guys stay close," she said, squatting down so she could be eye to eye with them. "And if you need anything, I'll be right up there in the stands, okay? You see my friend Kylie over there? The one in the orange Tigers jersey and the blue cowboy boots? She's waving at you."

The two kids looked and then nodded solemnly. Jamila shyly waved back at Kylie.

"I'll be sitting right next to her."

Already the crowds were streaming in, and the band was playing peppy music. Ava made her way toward the section of the bleachers where the AMS kids usually sat in a big clump. She passed Mr. Kelly, her neighbor, talking to some other man she didn't know.

He was in the midst of an animated conversation and didn't see her, which was just as well, because Ava was sure he didn't like her. He'd made it clear that he disapproved of a girl playing football, and he wasn't a fan of Coach's, either.

"Look there at those kids. You see those kids?" He was pointing toward Jamila and Shane.

The other man looked and nodded. "Yes, sir."

"That's no place for kids. It's dangerous for them and distracting for the players. I'm going to have words with Sackett after the game. He's too soft with Hardy. I think it's pink-slip time."

Ava hurried past and climbed into the bleachers, where she sat down next to Kylie.

"What does 'pink-slip time' mean?" asked Ava before she even said hello.

Kylie furrowed her brow. "Huh?"

Ava told her what she'd overheard Mr. Kelly say.

Kylie's frown deepened. "Giving someone a pink slip means firing them," she said grimly. "It sounds like Coach Byron's job is in trouble."

Ava had suspected it was something like that. Now she knew. "We have to do something," she said to Kylie. "He's such a good coach, and his kids are so cute. And—"

She broke off as Kylie grabbed her arm and gestured with her chin for Ava to look.

Ava turned.

Alex was standing down near the field, surrounded by a small crowd of gawking middle school kids. Two bright lights were shining on her, and a tech person was setting up a white screen on one side of her, which seemed to serve the purpose of reflecting the light onto her face. Her hair had been blown out until it was straight and shiny and un-Alex-looking, and even from a distance Ava could see that her twin had a ton of makeup on. She was wearing a smart blue blazer that Ava didn't recognize and was holding a microphone. A camera guy was fiddling with his camera, getting ready to shoot her. Next

69

to the cameraman stood an elegant woman in a red dress, wearing high-heeled red shoes. Her blond hair seemed to glow, and it must have had practically a full can of hair spray sprayed onto it, because not a strand moved when she moved her head. Ava knew it was Marcy Maxon. Next to Marcy stood a young woman talking on a cell phone, whom Ava guessed was the assistant, Candace.

"Why is Alex filming here at the high school game?" Kylie asked. "What's her story going to be about?"

"I don't know," said Ava. "She won't tell me. But it's been really hard to live with her. She's gotten all self-important about being a reporter. But it'll all be over after this weekend. Her story, whatever it is, is supposed to air on Sunday."

"That's good. Ooh, the game's starting!" said Kylie, pointing, as the Tigers kicked off.

"I know," said Ava, "and Alex isn't even *watching* it." She rolled her eyes, and then forgot about Alex as she turned to watch the game.

The Tigers won, but just barely. The score was tied 14–14 with two minutes to go. The Tigers managed to move the ball into field goal position, and with eighteen seconds left on the clock, Winston Schmidt kicked a field goal to win it, 17–14.

"Are you going to Sal's?" yelled Kylie over the roar of the crowd and the victory music of the band.

"I think so!" Ava shouted back. "But I'm going to talk to Alex first!"

Before she found her sister, Ava went to check on Jamila and Shane. When she spotted them sitting obediently on the bench near their dad, she set off toward Alex, who was standing near the concession area, talking on her phone. The film crew was no longer with her.

"Okay, yes, tomorrow at nine thirty, main gate. See you then. Bye." Alex clicked off her phone and jumped backward in surprise when she saw Ava. "Oh! Hi!" she said. "Didn't see you there."

Ava crossed her arms and narrowed her eyes. "Who was that?" she asked.

"Who was what?"

"On the phone. The person you were talk-ing to."

"Oh! Ha-ha! That was Marcy. She told me to call her that, by the way. In showbiz, people call each other by their first names. Hey, are we going to Sal's?"

"*Where* are you meeting her tomorrow morning at nine thirty?" asked Ava, ignoring Alex's attempt to change the subject.

Alex shifted from one foot to the other and looked everywhere but at Ava. Her hair, like Marcy's, didn't move when she moved her head.

"Um, yeah," said Alex. "About tomorrow. I was actually going to bring it up with you."

Ava stood and waited.

"See, I know you said you didn't want me to do the story about you?" Alex was speaking quickly. "But then when you decided to sit out? Suddenly I realized—wow. This would make an even better story than when the whole team wasn't going to play." She stared over Ava's head and made a movie screen with her hands, her thumbs touching. "The triumph of the human spirit. The sacrifice of the individual in the service of the common good." She dropped her hands. "And I knew you'd understand that it's kind of a once-in-a-lifetime opportunity for me, my big break. As a reporter. It's practically

Pulitzer Prize material. So I told Marcy—"

"But I told you I didn't want you to do the story about me," said Ava in a low, steely voice.

"Yes, yes, I know, but that was before, when the game was a forfeit. Of *course* you wouldn't want me to do a story when no game was played, because how boring would that be, right? Ha! Ha!"

Ava didn't laugh.

"Aaaaanyway," Alex continued in a singsong voice, "I figured now that there's going to *be* a game, you'd see how awesome it would be, um." Alex stopped and swallowed. "And, um, I talked it over with my production team and my crew, and they—"

"I'm your sister. What's more important? Your production team or me?" Ava felt hot, angry tears spring to her eyes. How could Alex betray her like this? And then the realization hit her: Alex had actually talked her into sitting out the game. Was it so that Alex could do this story? That whole speech she'd given Ava about doing it for the sake of her teammates, and all along, Alex's secret motivation had been to talk Ava into it so she could report her dumb story. Ava was so angry she couldn't say anything.

Alex seemed suddenly to be at a loss for words. She opened her mouth to say something, and then closed it again, her eyes pleading with Ava not to be angry.

Ava turned her back on Alex. "I can't stop you from doing the story, but I told you how I feel. Do what you feel you have to do," she said bitterly, and left Alex standing there.

CHAPTER NINE

At nine thirty the next morning, Alex stood by herself at the main gate leading to the middle school football field, waiting for the film crew to show up for the Briar Ridge game. Spectators were already filing past her, carrying programs and portable bleacher seats. Even at this early hour, the crowd seemed much larger than was typical for an Ashland Middle School game, and Alex supposed that the news of Ava's situation had attracted curious fans from both sides. Neither she nor Ava had ended up going to Sal's the night before, and they hadn't spoken to each other at breakfast that morning. If their parents had noticed, they hadn't said anything about it.

Alex spotted the white news van pulling in, and her heart began to pound. She watched it park, and then Marcy stepped out from the front passenger side, looking breathtaking in a green dress with oversize pearls and complicated-looking black, strappy, high-heeled sandals. It wasn't the sort of outfit one saw at a middle school football game very often. Marcy led the way toward the front entrance gate, stepping gingerly on the cracked and pebble-strewn asphalt. Behind her followed the cameraman, sound guy, lighting person, and Candace the assistant, like a line of ducklings trailing a mother duck.

"Hi, Marcy," said Alex in a small voice as they reached her. She nodded to the rest of the crew. Candace took a phone call.

"Hello, Alexandra," said Marcy. She flashed her thousand-watt TV smile. Alex marveled at how bright white her teeth were. "Are we ready to film Eva's game?"

"Um, actually, that's what I wanted to talk to you about," said Alex in a tiny voice. "I'm afraid we can't."

Candace snapped her phone off and stared at Alex in disbelief. "I knew nothing about this," she said to Marcy.

Marcy's smile evaporated. "What's the problem, Alexandra?"

Behind her, the other crew members exchanged uneasy glances with one another.

"Um, you can call me Alex?" said Alex. When Marcy didn't respond, she continued. "You see, my sister, *Ava*, doesn't want me to do this story about her. I thought I could talk her into it, but I realized I can't."

Marcy crossed her arms and stared down at Alex with a deeply unhappy look. "And you decided to wait to the last minute to tell us this—why?" she asked. All hint of cheer had drained from her voice.

"I'm really, really sorry that you came all this way," said Alex. "Honestly, when I got here, I was planning to just do the story anyway and try to make it up to Ava later. But I can't do that to my sister. We're twins. We're best friends. I need to take her feelings into account, and I just—I didn't realize just how strongly she felt."

Marcy nodded. "Well then, I guess we'll just pack up and go," she said. "But you do understand, Alexandra, that your story is supposed to air on the five o'clock news tomorrow night. I'm not sure what you have in mind for another idea, but your time is almost running out."

"I think her time has already run out," said Candace in a low voice. "I say we run that dancing parrot story."

Marcy shook her head impatiently. Her perfect eyebrows furrowed and she tapped her shoe, considering the situation. Alex could see ruby-red lacquer on Marcy's toes. "No, let's not kill the story yet," she said, half to Candace and half to herself. "I'll give her an hour to think of something. We'll see how she does under real-life deadline pressure."

Candace glanced at Alex, sniffed haughtily, and checked her phone for messages.

"Alexandra," said Marcy in a steely tone, "I need to warn you that if you can't come up with a quick idea for a *good* story, we'll need to fill that airtime with other programming. My boss, the head of the station, is not going to be pleased to hear this. People love the 'Tomorrow's Reporters Today' segment."

Alex nodded tearfully. Her chin quivered. "I know. I'm sorry. I'll think of something," she said.

Candace speed-dialed a number and mumbled something darkly to the person who answered. Marcy gave Alex a last reproachful look and then turned her back on her. Alex watched them head back to their news wagon and drive off. Then she slumped against the chain-link fence, staring down at her sneakers. A huge lump rose in her throat. Her career as a Pulitzer Prize–winning reporter was finished before it had even started.

"Hey there, Ms. Sackett," said a smooth, friendly voice.

She jerked her chin up. Luke! She quickly wiped her eyes and tried to smile.

"Heading to your sister's game?" he asked. He was wearing an Ashland Tigers T-shirt and a backward baseball cap.

"What game? Oh! Yes! Of course I am!" she said breathlessly. "I wouldn't miss it. Are you going?"

"Yup," he said. "So have you started *David Copperfield* yet?"

"Who? Oh! Um, not quite. I have so much homework right now," she said lamely. In fact, she hadn't even looked at it. The night before she'd accidentally dropped the huge book on her toe, which still hurt.

Luke peered at her. "Everything okay with you? You look a little glum."

Alex blinked a few times and smiled bravely.

"Oh, yeah, you know, reporter stuff," she said. "It's all good."

Luke nodded, looking a little unconvinced.

He's so sensitive, Alex thought. So in touch with her feelings. It was another sign they were meant to be together.

"Yeah, I wouldn't dream of missing my little pal's game," he said. "It's a shame what Briar Ridge is doing, but I'm proud of her for taking ownership of her decision."

Alex swallowed down the lump in her throat. "Me too," she said.

"I'm also meeting Tom here," he added. "And then we'll head over to rehearsal afterward."

Alex had almost forgotten about Tommy's concert in all the drama that had unfolded.

"So I'll see you there tonight, right?" asked Luke over his shoulder.

"Yes!" she said. Once again, he was double-checking that she'd be there. For sure he was going to ask her to Homecoming. She watched him walk away, admiring the way his broad shoulders swung with each step.

And then an idea hit her like a bolt of lightning. She called after Luke.

"Hey!" she yelled.

He turned.

"Do you think Tommy and his trio would mind if I showed up at rehearsal too?"

He gave her the thumbs-up. "I'm sure they'd love it," he said. "Another person to practice for. See ya there."

Leave it to Luke to be the person to inspire her! Of course it would be him! She almost leaped into the air with joy. She had the best story idea ever!

Alex clicked her phone on and scrolled down to Marcy Maxon's number.

Ava turned around to view the crowd in the bleachers. It was the largest crowd they'd had at any game all season. Coach K had told her to get suited up, even though she was going to spend the game on the bench today. At first she'd thought that was weird, but now she was glad to be wearing her uniform. It made her feel more like a part of the team. And it made her stand out less. She hated standing out.

She spotted Alex. But where was the TV crew? She watched as Alex climbed up into the bleachers to sit with the rest of their family. Had she told the TV people not to come?

A movement in the parking lot caught her eye. A news vans was pulling in. But it was from Channel 7, a competing local station. And then another van pulled in, and another, in a caravan formation. The only crew she *didn't* see was the white KHXA van. Well, it seemed the media had found out about the controversy. From the size of the crowds in the stands, she supposed she wasn't surprised.

Suddenly Alex was behind her, calling to her from the fence. Ava stood up and trotted over to her.

"Ave," said Alex. "I know this looks bad. I know it looks like I'm doing the story about you even though you didn't want me to. But I just told Marcy I'm not going to do it. I sent her away."

"Was she mad?" asked Ava.

Alex nodded. "Yeah, she was furious. But I told her you're more important."

"Thanks, Al," said Ava.

"The thing is," said Alex, "I don't know how all these other reporters found out. I did not tell anyone besides Marcy."

Ava looked at all the TV vans lined up in the

parking lot. She shrugged. "I guess this game is big news in this town."

"I guess so," said Alex. "Anyway, I had another idea for a story, and you're not in it, I promise. I'll tell you about it after the game."

Ava smiled. "Okay. Thanks."

"Good luck with everything," said Alex, and they touched knuckles with each other through the fence.

Ava returned to the bench to watch the last few minutes of warm-ups, feeling relieved that Alex had finally listened to her, although still a little angry that it had taken her this long. Corey came over and sat down next to her. "Did you see the Briar Ridge cheerleaders?" he asked her, gesturing toward the other side of the field.

Ava leaned out from the bench and looked past him. There they were, a line of cheerleaders dressed in the Briar Ridge colors—crimson and white—but what were they *doing*? They were just *sitting* there, literally. Sitting on the ground, their pom-poms carefully aligned in a neat row in front of them, with their hands in their laps, watching the warm-ups. They seemed cheerful enough, chatting and laughing with one another, but they weren't *cheering*.

"What's going on?" asked Ava. "Why are they just sitting there? And since when do cheerleaders wearing crimson and white sport huge pink bows in their hair? Even I know those colors don't go together."

"They're staging a demonstration. I guess it's what you might call a sit-in," said Corey. "To protest the fact that their team won't play against a team with a girl. They're on your side, Sackett," he added with a grin. "The pink bows are for you."

Ava stared harder. This was a revelation of sorts. For the first time, it occurred to her that maybe not everyone from Briar Ridge School felt the same way.

Bryce trotted over to where Corey and Ava were sitting. "Hey," he said. "Did you see what's on their helmets?"

Ava looked. Her eyes widened. The Briar Ridge team had pink heart stickers stuck to the backs of their otherwise crimson-colored helmets.

"'Pro-girl,' their kicker told me those were," said Bryce. "Seems like the kids all wanted to play against you. I guess it's the parents and the administrators that are the problem. The kids couldn't have cared less."

"What's your sister up to?" asked Corey.

Ava looked. Alex was making her way down the bleacher stairs. Ava knew her sister well enough to recognize that Alex was on a mission. Ava watched her run over to Lindsey and Emily, who had just finished a cheer routine. Alex and Lindsey and Emily and the rest of the Tiger Cub cheerleaders formed a huddle.

"She and Rosa are heading toward the Briar Ridge cheerleaders," said Bryce. "What for?"

"No clue," said Ava. They watched Alex and Rosa Navarro, the Ashland cheerleaders' seventh-grade captain, stoop down to speak to the Briar Ridge cheerleaders.

Alex beckoned to the AMS squad. The rest of the AMS cheerleaders approached the Briar Ridge cheerleaders, who all began moving over. The AMS squad sat down among them. Alex did too.

"Our cheerleaders are joining the protest," said Corey, chuckling. "Good for them."

It didn't surprise Ava that Alex would be part of the mix. After all, she *was* the public relations director for the cheer team. Ava was sure that joining forces with the opposing team's cheerleaders had been Alex's idea. It was just the sort of thing Alex would think of. The cynical part of her wondered if Alex was behind this protest just for the sake of her news story, but she dismissed that thought. Marcy Maxon's TV crew wasn't there to film it.

The television crews all seem to have realized what was going on at the same moment, because Ava saw several of them point, gather up their stuff, and go running toward where the cheerleaders were all sitting down. Cameras flashed, videos were turned on, and newscasters bent down awkwardly to interview the girls.

The Colts won the toss. The Tiger Cubs lined up to kick off. Bryce Hobson raised his hand to signal he was ready to kick. Ava felt a twinge of bitterness. That should be her, Ava, kicking off. The refs blew the whistle, and the game began.

CHAPTER TEN

The game was close, a defensive battle. Both teams had trouble getting the ball into the opponent's red zone, but toward the end of the first half, Corey connected with Owen on a fly pattern, and Owen ran it in for a touchdown.

And then Bryce missed the extra point. Ava, sitting so close to the edge of the bench that she kept almost falling off, tried not to show any emotion when the kick went wide. She knew Bryce was feeling a lot of pressure, especially as his opening kickoff had gone out of bounds. And she also knew he didn't need an emotional reaction from her to add to his stress.

With about a minute left in the first half, the

Briar Ridge quarterback dropped back to pass, couldn't find anyone, scrambled, and ran it in for a touchdown. At halftime, the score was 7–6, Briar Ridge. Even though she was focused on the game, Ava couldn't help but notice that the cheerleaders from both sides remained quietly sitting, side by side, even after their teams scored. It was very strange to see.

Ava gathered her helmet up and headed with her team toward the locker room, falling into step beside Xander.

"You hear what they're chanting?" he asked her.

She looked at him, startled. She'd been so caught up in what she was going to say to Bryce to help him straighten out his kicking motion, she hadn't been paying attention to the chant that had begun in the Ashland stands and spread to the opposing side as well.

"Ay-VUH! Ay-VUH! Ay-VUH! Ay-VUH!"

Then she became aware that several newspeople were walking at a distance from the team, but keeping pace with her, snapping pictures.

Coach K looked up from his clipboard at the door of the locker room. "Well, you'd better acknowledge your fans, Sackett," he said gruffly.

She looked at him in alarm, and then turned toward the bleachers and awkwardly waved to the crowd.

A huge cheer went up. Cameras started flashing like crazy. She ducked into the locker room.

During his halftime tirade (halftime was the only time Ava went into the boy's locker room), Coach K did not acknowledge the media or the cheerleader protest, and Ava was grateful for that. He mostly bellowed about the need to gang-tackle on defense and better protect the quarterback on offense.

As the AMS kick return team trotted onto the field at the start of the second half, Ava glanced again at all the cheerleaders. The news teams were still snapping pictures and attempting to get the girls to speak to the cameras. Alex was no longer in their midst, but Ava became absorbed in the game before she had time to wonder where her twin had gone.

Neither team could move the ball in the third quarter, but in the fourth quarter, with seconds remaining in the game, the Cubs made it to the five yard line. Corey pitched the ball to Greg Fowler, the running back, who sprinted wide behind some blockers. At the one yard line, he dove for the end zone and touched the ball down just inside the goal line before tumbling out of bounds.

Ava clutched the edge of the bench tightly and waited. Was this a repeat of last year? Would it be ruled a touchdown? Had Greg gotten the ball across the line before he went out of bounds?

The crowd held its collective breath.

The ref's arms shot up.

Touchdown. The Cubs were ahead 12–7 and the clock read 0 seconds left to play.

The Ashland side roared and cheered. Then everyone's eyes focused on the cheerleaders. How would *they* respond?

Ava looked too. They were all standing up now. The Briar Ridge and Ashland cheerleaders were all standing together in a long line, linking elbows. *A sign of unity?* Ava wondered. Cameras flashed. The cheerleaders were definitely as big a story as the game being played on the field.

After the game, Ava walked with her team

toward the locker room. As the rest of her team-mates veered to the left to go change in the boys' lockers, Ava turned to the right and stopped short. A big crew of reporters was standing in front of the doorway to the girls' locker room, waiting for her. Her heart sank. They barricaded the doorway, trying to force her to stop to talk, but she didn't want to talk.

"Ava! Ava!" They all shouted questions at her. "Can you tell us about your decision to sit out? How do you feel about the fact that the game was played without you? Did you know about the cheerleaders' protest ahead of time?"

Her father appeared out of nowhere and took Ava by the elbow.

"Let her into the locker room, please," Coach said, cordially but firmly.

Ava's heart swelled with gratitude to her father. How had he known they'd be there?

As she entered, she glanced behind to see the reporters swarming around Coach.

"Coach Sackett! How do you feel about your daughter not being permitted to play?"

"Was it her idea or yours that she sit this one out?"

"Will this hurt Briar Ridge players in future

recruiting decisions made by you and your staff?"

The voices faded away as the door to Ava's locker room closed.

Alex locked her bike to a conveniently located bike rack, and then headed around to the side of a building, to the black stage door of the Press, as Tommy had instructed her. Inside it was dark after the bright sun outside, and her eyes took a minute to adjust. When they did, she found herself standing in a dim entryway. The black-painted wood floor was battered and scuffed. A velvet-curtained doorway led the way up a short flight of wooden steps to the performance area. She could hear music playing. Amazing music. She recognized Tommy's piano part, having heard him practicing on his keyboard practically every night. But it sounded so much better on a real piano. No wonder he kept hounding their parents for one.

Alex rechecked her message from Marcy Maxon. Marcy had been lukewarm about Alex's new idea, to do her piece about Tommy and his trio, but at least she hadn't said no. Alex clicked through to read the text for the tenth time:

> It's not as strong as the football story. But I'm willing to send my crew to film. If you can frame it as "Coach Sackett's son, the artist born into an athletic family," well then, possibly. But if I don't think the piece is good enough to air, I want you to know I won't hesitate to kill it.

Alex cringed at the last sentence. Did journalists have to use violent metaphors like "kill"? She swallowed. This would have to be a good story.

The music ended just as she poked her head through the side curtain. Tommy looked up. "Yo, Alex!" he called. "Come meet my partners in crime. This is Harley and that's Jackson."

Harley twirled her big double bass on its metal foot, and then turned and smiled at Alex.

Forget Marcy Maxon! Alex immediately decided that her new ambition was to look, dress, and act exactly like Harley by the time she was in high school, if not sooner. She goggled at

the girl, abashed by her beauty, her sophistication, and her easy manner.

Harley was tall and slender in black jeans,
black cowboy boots, a white T-shirt, and a
slim-fitting, buttery-soft-looking black leather
jacket. Her long, glossy brown hair was pulled
back into a casual ponytail, revealing a finely
chiseled face with no discernible makeup
besides ruby-red lips. Her dark eyes were as
large as a fawn's, her brows thick and even.

"H-h-hi!" said Alex, suddenly overcome with
shyness.

"Looks like your sister inherited all the good
looks in the family, bro," said Jackson with a
little chuckle.

Alex tore her eyes away from Harley and said
hello to Jackson. She realized she'd seen both
Jackson and Harley once before, when they'd
come to play at her parents' anniversary dinner a few weeks before. But it had been dark
and somewhat chaotic in the restaurant when
dozens of people had shown up to wish them
a happy anniversary, so she hadn't really paid
much attention. Now she was able to get a
good look at Jackson, sitting casually behind his
drum set, and he, too, struck her as the height

of sophistication. He had dark skin and close-cropped hair, and in spite of the dim lighting, wore tiny oblong-shaped sunglasses, which emphasized his handsome face. He had on a pale-green shirt and faded jeans, and there was a gold stud in one ear.

She'd almost forgotten to look for Luke, but a quick scan of the small, ultrahip seating area told her he wasn't in the room. About a dozen tiny tables were arranged near the performance area, and behind them she could make out racks of books, magazines, and cards. Along one wall was a polished wooden counter and gleaming coffee-making equipment. She could hear some banging and talking coming from a room beyond a door and presumed it led to a kitchen. They were probably prepping for the evening, she decided.

"Are you a musician like your brother?" asked Harley, smiling at Alex.

"Me? Oh, ah-ha-ha, no, not really," said Alex, immediately resolving to take up an instrument as soon as possible. "Did my brother tell you why I was here?"

"You're doing a story about us," said Jackson. He gave her a thumbs-up. "That is cool." He drew out the last word in a very charming way.

"Yes, and I thought I'd just come to rehearsal to listen and to figure out what I can talk about with you tonight when my crew shows up. I'm thinking that I'll start with an intro, and then you perform a song, and then after the show maybe I can interview all three of you together."

"Sounds like a plan," said Tommy. Then he looked past Alex. "Oh, hey, Luke." He elbowed Alex. "Al, come meet our manager."

CHAPTER ELEVEN

It took every nerve fiber in Alex's body to stay calm, look unperturbed, and turn around with a casual "Oh, hi!" She managed it, but barely. In spite of her cool exterior, she felt her pulse racing and her stomach turning.

Luke was still dressed as he'd been that morning, in his backward hat, Ashland shirt, athletic shorts, and sneakers. *But he could wear a burlap sack and still look like the perfect man,* Alex thought.

Luke smiled at Alex and greeted the others.

Was he trying not to reveal the depth of his emotions? Was he using every reserve of his strength to hide his passionate feelings from his friends? How bravely he was behaving! Well, if he could be brave, so could she.

"Go sit in the back," Tommy ordered him. "Let us know how it sounds from there."

"Will do," agreed Luke. He wound his way through the little seating area and sat down at a table that was the farthest from the performance space.

"You go too, Al," said Tommy. "Tell us if the balance sounds right. We haven't done an actual sound check yet, but the guy will be here soon."

Alex gulped, but obediently made her way toward the back table where Luke was sitting, avoiding her gaze for fear of betraying his love. "Be cool, be cool, be cool," she said under her breath.

Tommy and Harley and Jackson began to play.

Alex hadn't even pulled the chair out when her phone buzzed. A text. From Ava.

> Al, where are you? I need to talk
> to you right away. It's important.
> I'm at the park near our house.
> Please come?

What could that mean? Ava was not one to be overly dramatic. It really must be important. Alex texted back:

> Okay. I have my bike with me.
> Be there in ten.

With an apologetic look, she turned to Luke. "I have to go, sorry. Ava needs me. But I'll see you here tonight?"

"Sounds good," said Luke, but he barely glanced at her. He was pretending to be engrossed in the music.

Fine, Alex thought. *Better not to make a scene.*

As she turned to go, though, he suddenly stood up and put a hand on her arm, sending electric sparks shooting down to her fingertips. "Hey, Al? Can I ask you something?"

Now was the moment. He was going to ask her to Homecoming. She stood stock-still, breathing shallow breaths.

The music stopped.

"How does that sound?" Tommy yelled to Luke and Alex.

They both turned.

"Great!" called Alex, but it came out a little squeaky. She felt as though she and Luke had been caught doing something they shouldn't.

"Harley needs to move the mike closer," Luke called, not sounding a bit nervous or guilty. "Her low notes are getting swallowed."

Alex turned and stared at him with newfound admiration. He knew about music, too? What *didn't* this guy do well?

Luke seemed to read her thoughts. "I'm just an amateur," he said modestly. "But they asked me to be their manager because I have a good ear and I'm pretty good at sound mixing and stuff. I helped them put together their EP."

"That's so cool," she breathed. "So what were you going to ask me?"

"Oh! Right. Okay, I know this is weird. Not the sort of thing a guy my age should ask a girl your age. But you're pretty mature for stuff like this."

"Yes! I am!" Alex blurted out. Then she mentally kicked herself. *Don't keep interrupting him.*

"So what I want to ask is a surprise, and . . . I know this is your big story and all, but when you introduce the band on camera tonight, can you also introduce me? You know, as the band's manager? And then I'll ask a quick question. It—it has to do with Homecoming. You can probably guess what I'm going to do. But I promise not to mess up your story."

She looked into his summer-sky-blue eyes, soft and dewy and slightly pleading. She couldn't say no to those eyes, even if she wanted to. Which she didn't. "Of—of course," she managed to say. "No problem! I'll be ready!"

"You're the best," he said, and gave her a quick hug, which left her gasping for air.

As she bicycled toward Ava and the park near their house, she wanted to scream with joy at the top of her lungs, but barely restrained herself. Luke was going to ask her to Homecoming *on camera*! What a story this was turning out to be!

Ava paced up and down, up and down, scanning the corner for Alex to appear. What was taking her so long? It had been more than fifteen minutes since Alex had texted that she was coming. And Alex was *never* late.

Ten more minutes went by, but at last she saw her sister round the corner on her blue bike, her silver helmet gleaming in the afternoon sun.

Alex rode through the open gate and skidded to a stop near Ava. She hopped off, leaning her bike against the fence. "What's up?" she asked, panting slightly as she took off her helmet and shook out her long hair. "That was a strange message you sent."

"What took you so long?" asked Ava. "You're never late."

"Oh, yeah, sorry," said Alex, and she blushed to the roots of her hair. "I was unavoidably detained by—well, tell me what's up first, and then I'll tell you why I was late. Why couldn't I just meet you at home?"

"Because it's about Coach Byron," said Ava. "I didn't know what to do. I was just at home with Coach and Mom, and I swear I wasn't listening on purpose, but I was carrying a basket of laundry downstairs and I heard them talking in the kitchen. I guess Mr. Kelly went to the athletic director and demanded that Coach fire Coach Byron for missing so many practices."

Alex gasped. "No! He can't!"

"Well, yes he can, actually. I heard Coach tell

Mom that he doesn't think there's anything he can really do about it, that he sort of has to fire him because he's not fulfilling his obligations, and he's going to have a talk with him Monday morning." Tears welled up in Ava's eyes, and she swallowed down a lump in her throat. "I'd babysit for his kids every second if I could, but football takes up so much time, and the times they need babysitting—during high school practices—are usually at the same time as *my* practices. I want to do something, though, Al. I love those kids."

Alex put a hand on Ava's shoulder. "That's bad," she agreed. "You're right. We need to do something. Let's sit on the swings so I can think."

The park was empty, and the girls sat down side by side on the swing set. It brought back memories for Ava of endless hours swinging together in their backyard in Massachusetts. Ava had always been the daredevil, swinging as high as she could and leaping off.

Now they sat quietly, barely moving. Ava could almost see the wheels turning in Alex's brain. Alex was so good at organizing and strategizing, way better than Ava. And Ava knew Alex adored Shane and Jamila too. Plus, Ava still felt like Alex really owed her one after almost going ahead with her news story about Briar Ridge when Ava had asked her not to.

"Let me ponder this a little more," said Alex at last. "It sounds like nothing's going to happen before Monday. We have a little time to come up with a plan."

"Okay," said Ava, feeling a tiny bit better, but still wishing Alex had jumped into action like she normally did. "Thanks for coming. Now tell me where you were, and why you were late."

Alex swiveled her swing so she was facing Ava and told her about her new idea for her story. "Tommy's trio is so good, Ave. And they're all really good-looking, so they'll look great on television. It's the perfect piece. Marcy mentioned something about interviewing Coach, too, about his son playing piano and football, but I don't think Tommy will mind. The story will be great publicity for the trio."

Ava nodded. Her suspicions about Marcy Maxon were growing. It really did seem as though Marcy's main priority was to use Alex to get to Coach, from whatever angle she could. First she'd wanted the story to be about Coach's daughter, denied the right to play football. Now it was Coach's son, the misunderstood artist forced by circumstances to be a football player. Well, maybe their mom was right. Everyone could use an angle. If this was a good way to get publicity for Tommy's trio, then maybe Marcy's motives in using Alex didn't matter.

"Ava, I know I owe you a gigantic apology," said Alex. She hung her head. "You were right. I *did* want you to sit out so I could do my piece. Marcy asked me to, and I was so anxious to get a good story that I forgot that sisters come first. I'm really sorry, Ave."

Ava stared at her sister. She couldn't exactly say she was surprised to hear this, but still. Her suspicions about Alex's motives had been right. But she brushed it off. Maybe Alex had swayed her decision, but Ava didn't want to believe that she, Ava, had allowed Alex to be the deciding factor. She shook her head. "*I* made the decision not to play," she said. "Maybe what you said got me to decide sooner than I would have, but I think I would have decided not to play no matter what, because the game meant so much to my team. And I'm glad that I did. Because by not playing, I called attention to how stupid the Briar Ridge administration was, and it got a ton of press, and Coach K told me that now it's become a huge issue at the school, and there's a whole group of other parents who want the school to apologize to Ashland Middle School and to me. So even though it stunk that I couldn't play, I'm glad it turned out the way it did."

"I'm glad too," said Alex. "Even if Marcy Maxon did get mad at me for deciding not to do the story on you."

"Well, I'm sure this one is going to turn out great," said Ava, more stiffly than she meant to. All of what she had just said was true, but she was still feeling a little stunned and hurt by Alex's confession. *This might take me some time to get over,* she realized.

"Thanks, Ave," said Alex. Her eyes suddenly sparkled. "Okay, so now I'll tell you why I was late. I have huge, I mean, *huge* news. Remember I told you about the guy who has a crush on me?"

Ava nodded warily.

"Well, he just asked me if I would mind if he asked me to Homecoming *on camera* tonight."

Ava stared at Alex. "That's crazy! Who is it? Will you tell me now?" *Please don't let her say Luke,* Ava thought, as hard as she could.

Alex clutched Ava's arm with two hands.

"Luke! Luke Grabowski!" She let out a little squeal and did a delighted back-and-forth swoop on her swing.

Ava groaned and put her head in her hands. "It can't be," she said. "That's impossible."

Alex's smile evaporated, and she made her swing stop dead. "Why is it impossible? It's impossible that he would want to ask me to Homecoming?"

"Well, yeah, kind of," said Ava. "Al, it's pretty clear you've had a crush on him since the first time you laid eyes on him, but I really, really don't think it's mutual. Trust me on this one."

"Well, I *don't* trust you on this one," said Alex. "Because he told me he's going to ask me. So there."

"But last time he came over, he told me he had a crush on someone."

"I know," said Alex. "On me. Duh. For obvious reasons, he didn't tell you who it was."

Now doubt was creeping into Ava's mind. Could it really be that Luke liked Alex? "But Al, he's my *tutor*! Ew!"

"This isn't about you, Ave. He's not *my* tutor. We have a separate relationship. We talk about books, and—and, well, coffee."

"But he's three grades older than you are. What exactly did he say to you?"

"He asked me if I would mind introducing him tonight, along with Tommy and Harley and Jackson," Alex said frostily. "Because he's the band's manager. And then he asked if I would mind if he asked me to Homecoming on camera. I won't even tell Marcy it's going to happen. She'll love it. It'll make a great story. We're sort of a Romeo and Juliet couple."

"Romeo and Juliet?" repeated Ava, and a snort escaped from her.

Now Alex looked quite indignant. She stood up from her swing and crossed her arms. "Yes, we are. Because the whole entire world is trying to keep us apart. Mom doesn't want me to come near him when the two of you are working together. You tell me he's too old for me, which he is not. Even Tommy tried to interrupt a conversation we were having. But I don't care what the world thinks. We were meant to be together."

Ava was stunned. Was Alex delusional? Luke hadn't shown the slightest sign that he was interested in Alex when Ava had been around the two of them. And Alex had certainly been known to misunderstand things like this in the past. "Listen, Al. Should I come to the Press tonight? I know Tommy said he didn't want the whole family coming because that would seem dorky, but maybe I should be there to, ah, to support you?"

"That won't be necessary," said Alex primly.

Ava could tell her twin was mad at her. "Okay, well, I'll have my phone nearby in case you need me."

"I won't need you," Alex snapped. "Now I have to go get changed and do my makeup for the shoot." She shoved her helmet on her head and stalked off.

Ava watched her climb on her bike and ride away.

CHAPTER TWELVE

Alex sat in the car and took some cleansing breaths. "Do I look okay, Mom?"

Mrs. Sackett stared at Alex and reached out to touch a lock of her shiny, newly straightened hair. "You look beautiful, honey. I'm not really used to seeing you, so, um, camera-ready, but I guess I'll have to get used to it if I'm going to be the mother of a famous TV reporter. Are you absolutely sure Daddy and I can't come in and see this?"

"No, sorry, Mom," said Alex. "Tommy gave strict instructions to make this about his group, and you know how Coach attracts attention wherever he goes. Plus, well, it's not exactly your crowd."

Mrs. Sackett sighed. "I can't believe we're about to have four celebrities in the family. First your father and his coaching, then your sister and her football, and now Tom, my famous musician son, and you, my famous reporter daughter."

"Well, you're going to break into the big time yourself, with your pottery," said Alex loyally.

The news van pulled up alongside the curb in front of them.

"They're here," said Alex. She blew her mom an air kiss. "Gotta go."

"Good luck, sweetie," said her mother, as Alex hopped out.

Marcy had on another stunning outfit, this one a formfitting, royal-blue sheath dress accessorized with a gold link necklace and knee-high patent-leather black boots. Alex immediately felt little-girlish in her black-and-white-striped tee and green skirt with flounces, but it was too late now. As she'd been getting dressed earlier, she'd thought her outfit looked older and more sophisticated than what she usually wore. But next to Marcy's, it seemed so immature.

Alex greeted Marcy and Candace and the rest of the crew and led the way through the stage-door entrance to where Tommy and Harley and Jackson were getting set up. Harley looked breathtaking in a short black dress with a halter-type neckline and slightly forties-style black pumps. Who was the movie actress her mom had pointed out a few Sunday movie nights ago? Lauren Bacall. That's who Harley resembled.

The place looked different than it had earlier that afternoon. The lighting was soft and romantic, and spotlights were beamed toward the stage area. Luke stood in the back near the coffee counter, consulting with a guy who looked like a sound technician.

The band began rehearsing a song. It had a saucy, swinglike beat. Alex gathered the crew together, out of earshot of the band, and spoke. "So I thought I would start by introducing the band members, and then you guys can shoot them playing a song or two?" She didn't mention Luke. She had a funny feeling Marcy would not approve of the plan to have him ask a surprise question on camera.

"All right, yes," said Marcy, "and what time is your father arriving?"

Candace took up her clipboard and held her pen poised above the schedule, waiting to hear Alex's response.

"Oh! Um, I don't think he'll be here," said Alex. "My brother didn't want our parents here."

Candace whispered something in Marcy's ear. Alex thought this was not very polite.

Marcy nodded at whatever it was Candace said, and then glared at Alex, tapping her toe. "This is not going well, Alexandra," she said.

"No, it really isn't," agreed Candace.

"You do realize that after you sent us away from your sister's game this morning, every other news station in the area showed up to cover the story except us?"

"Every other one," echoed Candace. "Even the *public* television station."

"I know."

"We were the *only* ones not there," Marcy continued. "It seems your decision to be a loyal sister has resulted in our missing out on a story."

"We really missed out," agreed Candace. "We got scooped."

"I know," said Alex. "I'm really sorry."

"And now, after I give you a second chance, you tell me that all we have to shoot here is your brother playing a few songs with his two friends? That's not a story, Alexandra." Marcy turned to Candace. "I don't think this is worth our staying for the show," she said in a low voice. "I'm thinking we should run that story about the dog rescued from the storm drain in this slot."

"What about the cat that likes to ride on the vacuum cleaner?"

"Hmm," reflected Marcy. "That might be good too."

Candace took out her phone to make a call.

Alex knew she had to think of something fast. "Wait!" she said, her mind racing. "What about the football angle?"

Marcy and Candace had already turned to leave, beckoning the cameraman, sound guy, makeup artist, and lighting woman to follow them, but at Alex's outburst Marcy held up a manicured hand, and everyone else stopped. They set their gear back down. Candace paused, her phone clamped under her chin.

"Well, Alexandra?" demanded Marcy. The others turned toward her expectantly.

"Okay, so we have footage from Friday night's game, right? Of Tommy in his football uniform and my dad coaching?"

"Yes," said Marcy. "But that's not very useful, is it, if we don't have an exclusive with Coach Sackett."

"No, it's not useful," agreed Candace, still holding her phone with her chin. "Not without an interview with her father."

"Wait, hear me out. So let me interview the trio, and we can approach the story from the angle that my brother is a musician who also plays football, like you said. And we can talk about how much he yearns to pursue his art, but was born into this family where he was destined to play football." Would Tommy mind if she brought football into this story? Alex wondered again. She really didn't think so. He was a lot less camera shy than Ava.

Marcy pursed her lips. "Hmm. Pretty thin. Now, if we could also talk about your twin sister who was born to play football but has been prevented by external forces from pursuing her dreams just because she's a girl, that might be a nice parallel. But we have no footage in the can of your sister and today's game."

Candace nodded. "Because you sent us away," she reminded Alex.

"I'll text Ava and see if she'll show up so I

can interview her," said Alex quickly. "She—she might." Would Ava show up?

Marcy turned to the crew and gave an almost imperceptible nod. They began unpacking their gear.

"All right, Alexandra," said Marcy. "We'll film the group and do the interview. But no promises. And I must tell you, my patience is wearing thin."

Ava was still in the park shooting baskets. It had been nearly two hours, though, and her stomach growled. She took it as a sign that it was time to go home to eat dinner.

As she unzipped her backpack to put away her ball, she noticed a text that had come in a while ago from Alex.

> Ava, can you please, please come to the Press as soon as humanly possible? I'll explain when you get here. Please?

Ava frowned down at her phone. So now Alex needed *her*? Ava had thought Alex didn't want anything to do with her tonight. And suddenly she was all "come right away, it's urgent" when she had been extremely casual about responding to Ava's urgent text earlier. Humph. Ava was still pretty upset with Alex, and she still didn't want to admit to herself that Alex's urging her to bow out so the game could be played actually *had* influenced her feelings about the whole thing. And now Alex needed her again, probably for this dumb news story. Was she planning to try to thrust Ava into the spotlight again in order to get a better story? Then there was the whole Luke issue. Luke was her tutor. Luke *couldn't* be interested in Alex. That seemed so wrong. On so many levels. She shuddered.

Ava reread the text and shook her head. The last thing she felt like doing was hopping on her bike and riding all the way to the Press in the growing darkness to bail Alex out of some harebrained scheme.

She decided to head home instead.

CHAPTER THIRTEEN

Alex checked her phone again. No response from Ava. And there was nothing she could do about Coach. There was no way he would show, especially after Tommy had asked him not to. Well, maybe Alex could convince Marcy that the footage they'd taken of Coach at the game would be good enough to "round out" the story.

"All right, Alexandra, we're ready," said Marcy. "Gather the band in and we'll have you start with your interview."

The trio must have been waiting for Marcy to say that, because they immediately stopped playing and headed over to the area where Marcy and her crew had set up the cameras and the lights. The audience members were filing in and taking their seats, but Candace was circulating around the room, asking people to be quiet and pointing to the camera crew.

The sound guy clipped a little microphone to Alex's collar and threaded it around behind her back, where he clipped a small black box to her skirt at the waist. Then he handed Alex a microphone with KHXA on it. The makeup lady zoomed in and fussed with Alex's hair. She whipped a can of hair spray out of the holster on her hip and sprayed a cloud of it over Alex, which made Alex cough. Then she did the same to Harley. She even dusted Tommy's and Jackson's faces with some sort of powder on a big, puffy brush.

Alex stood in the center of the group. On one side of her were Harley and Jackson. On the other was Tommy.

She felt a tiny bit nervous, but also strangely energized. She could see Luke waiting off to the side. Their eyes met, and he winked at her. She still hadn't told Marcy about including Luke in this interview. There was no sign of Ava, and Alex had a sinking feeling her twin wasn't coming. But she couldn't think about that now.

"Are you ready, Alexandra?" asked Marcy.

Alex nodded.

"Musicians?"

The three of them nodded.

"Audience?"

The people sitting in the café, which was now full to capacity, applauded quietly and were immediately shushed by Candace.

"All right, we're rolling," said the cameraman.

All nervousness left Alex. She smiled easily at the camera. "This is Alex Sackett, kid reporter for KHXA, and we're here at the Press in downtown Ashland, in front of a live audience with the hot new jazz trio of the moment!"

Her eyes flicked to Marcy. Marcy looked pleasantly surprised. Alex knew she was doing great. She was pretty sure she was a natural in front of the camera.

One by one, she introduced the band members, and asked each of them a question or two about themselves. When she got to Tommy, she asked, "So, Tom Sackett. You play piano for the group. And you're also a sophomore quarterback for the Ashland Tigers. How do you feel about your double life as an athlete and an artist?"

Marcy beamed and gave her a hearty, manicured thumbs-up.

"I love both music and sports," said Tommy. "I like to think I'm a combination of my twin sisters' passions. You're an artist, Alex, and our sister, Ava, is an athlete. Me? I'm both." He smiled charmingly.

Alex knew without turning her gaze that Luke was standing just off camera. Now was the moment. "Thanks, Tom. And yes, it's true we Sackett kids all inherited some combination of sports and artistic genes," she said with a winning smile. "But that's not all we think about! Some of us also have a romantic side. Luke, did you have something you wanted to add to this interview?" She beckoned to Luke to step into the shot, and he did so quickly, looking slightly ill at ease and holding something behind his back.

Alex could see Marcy's perfectly shaped eyebrows go up. Alex guessed she had been right in assuming the reporter was not a big fan of surprise appearances.

"Ladies and gentlemen, this is Luke Grabowski, the band's manager and producer. And he told me he would like to ask a question. Luke? What was it you wanted to ask?" Alex smiled encouragingly at him.

From behind his back, Luke drew out a bouquet of red roses wrapped in white tissue paper and tied with a pink ribbon.

Alex turned to smile into the camera, her heart fluttering. This was it!

"Thanks so much, Alex. I'll be quick here," said Luke. Then he turned from Alex to Harley. "Harley? Would you go to Homecoming with me?"

The smile on Alex's face froze. Disbelief swirled around her in a cloudy haze, so that suddenly she felt she couldn't see anything clearly or hear anything except faraway, muffled sounds. Had she heard correctly? Had Luke just asked *Harley* to Homecoming?

"I'd love to," came Harley's voice, and through the fog Alex watched her accept the bouquet Luke was holding out to her.

A moment later Luke stepped out of the shot, and Alex was still staring into the camera, frozen. Thoughts whooshed through her mind. Hadn't Tommy mentioned something about the "cute ask" contest for the high school Homecoming? Hadn't he told her how the person who asked a date in the most innovative and clever way would win some prize or other? Suddenly, like a person falling off a cliff whose life is zooming past in a rush, Alex's own mind recalled all the clues that should have told her it was Harley, not Alex, whom Luke wanted to ask to Homecoming. But she'd willfully ignored the signs. And now here she was, the classic deer in the headlights, unable to move or say or do anything. And the camera was rolling!

Somewhere in her clouded mind Alex was aware that too many seconds were ticking by, and Marcy was beginning to look alarmed. What was going on? Why had Alex stopped speaking?

Tommy must have also sensed something was amiss. Gently taking Alex by the wrist, he directed the microphone toward himself and cleared his throat.

"So, Alex!" he said cheerfully. "The one thing our band doesn't yet have is a name for our trio. We keep going back and forth, debating what would be best. We thought you might have an idea?"

Alex opened her mouth to speak, but all that came out was a sort of "gng-gnh."

"I have an idea!" said a voice just off camera.

Ava stepped into the shot and moved between Alex and Harley, so that the three Sackett kids were all next to one another. For a second they stood there, saying nothing. And then Ava stepped on Alex's toe. That seemed to restart her engine, and she found her voice. "This is my twin sister, Ava Sackett," she said. It was as though she were a windup train that had temporarily gone off track but had been set right again. She was back in the moment, smiling at the camera. "Ava, what's your suggestion for a name for the trio?"

Ava was wearing her AMS football jersey—without pads, of course—and had styled her hair and added a sparkly clip. Alex could see she was even wearing lip gloss!

"How about Trio Grande?" suggested Ava with a shy smile.

Tommy, Jackson, and Harley looked at one another and then at the camera. "That's awesome!" they said.

The audience applauded.

"And now, ladies and gentlemen," said Alex, back to her bold, confident self. "May I introduce— the Trio Grande!"

The audience burst into applause again, and the concert began.

CHAPTER
FOURTEEN

Ava sat at a little table close to the front of the room, listening to Tommy's trio perform as the television cameraman darted forward and backward, filming them from all angles. The trio was amazing. They played three numbers, all original compositions, which elicited enthusiastic clapping and cheering from the audience. Ava noticed that even Marcy Maxon seemed to be enjoying the music, tapping her high-heeled foot in time to the beat.

The applause was thunderous when they'd finished, and people flocked to the little table where Luke was selling the EP.

After the show, Ava joined Alex and the television crew outside. It was growing dark, but the lights from the café flooded the sidewalk in a golden glow. Tommy, Jackson, and Harley stood near the front entrance, surrounded by admirers and well-wishers.

"Ah, so here's the reclusive twin sister who doesn't like the spotlight," said Marcy when she saw Ava.

Ava wasn't sure if she was supposed to laugh at that or be offended. She acknowledged the comment with a little smile.

Marcy turned back to Alex and resumed what she had been saying. "The band is fantastic, no question," she said. "And now we've got footage of your twin sister, so that's good too. But we're missing an important angle—the Coach Sackett perspective. Without hearing from him, this piece feels incomplete. I'm sorry, Alexandra, but I just don't know if it's going to be compelling enough to run."

Ava saw Alex's face fall. Her chin began to quiver slightly, but if Marcy noticed, she did not acknowledge it. She gave her crew a little nod, and they began to fold up their equipment.

"Wait!" said Ava.

Everyone stopped and stared at her, including Alex.

"Please don't go yet," she said. "Wait here for just two more minutes. I'll be right back."

She didn't look back to see if they complied. She raced down the street, past three or four closed storefronts. She sped around the corner and stopped, panting. There he was.

"Coach! Wait up!"

Her father turned and waited for her to approach.

Panting, she grabbed his arm with both hands. "Coach, Alex needs you. Will you talk to her for her story, on camera?"

He frowned. "I promised Tom I wouldn't be a presence tonight for his big performance. It was fantastic to be able to listen to them from the stage-door entrance, and I'm grateful you got me there. But he doesn't know I was there, and I don't want to steal his spotlight."

"Coach. The concert is over. He'll understand. And we can ask him first to make sure. Just please, please come? For Alex?"

That seemed to clinch it. He followed her back to the Press.

Marcy Maxon glanced at her sparkly watch for the third time in three minutes. "I'm sorry, Alexandra," she said. "We need to get going. I have to edit the other story for tomorrow evening's slot."

Alex willed herself not to cry. "I understand," she said in a tiny voice. "I'm sorry it didn't work out."

"Marcy, look who's coming," said Candace, gesturing down the block.

Alex looked too. Ava was coming toward them at a race-walk pace, followed close behind by their dad. Alex held in a gasp.

"Well, well, well," said Marcy. "It seems we might just have an angle after all."

Coach shook hands with Marcy and the rest of her crew. "I understand you need a statement," he said with a wry smile.

"Coach Sackett!" said Marcy, in a breathy voice. "How nice of you to join us! Yes, we would be delighted if Alexandra could conduct a quick interview with you on your thoughts about Tom being a musician."

Marcy's whole demeanor had transformed. Suddenly she was all smiles and seemed a little abashed to be in Coach's presence, as though he were a movie star or something. Sometimes Alex forgot that her dad had this effect on people.

"Sure," said Coach. "Where would you like us to stand?"

"Wait!" said Alex.

Everyone turned.

"I need to get Tom's permission," she said. "After all, this is his story."

"You're right, Alex," said Coach. "Go ask him."

Of course Tommy was fine with it. "Heck yeah," he said. "This piece of yours has been the best free publicity anyone could ask for!"

By this time Tommy, Harley, and Jackson had joined the rest of the group outside the café. Their well-wishers moved over to the interview area to watch.

The cameraman gave the signal, and Alex stood side by side with her father. She beamed into the camera, once again feeling electrified and euphoric as soon as the little red light went on.

"We're rolling," said the cameraman.

"So, Coach Sackett, I mean, Dad," said Alex, "how do you feel about your son pursuing his artistic dream?"

"I'm proud of him. Truly, deeply happy that he's become the person that he is." Coach was also very relaxed in front of the camera. This didn't surprise Alex, of course, as he'd been mobbed by the press ever since he'd accepted the position of coach of the Tigers, and he'd done dozens upon dozens of interviews.

"And what if one day soon, your son chooses music over football? How will you feel then?" It was a question Alex had been longing to ask her father for some time now. How weird that she was finally asking it of him here, in front of a crowd and with a camera rolling.

Everyone waited to hear what Coach would say.

Coach considered the question. "I've said this to my children many times: Sports don't matter. And yet, they matter a great deal. That's a paradox we live with." He beckoned to Tommy with a finger, and Tommy wove his way through the little crowd until he was standing before the camera alongside Alex and their father. Ava stepped into the frame as well, and Coach put an arm around Tommy's shoulder. "I have chosen to pursue a path where sports matter a great deal. But my one hope for my children, besides good health, is that they choose to pursue a path that leads to a rich and satisfying life. Not just the life of the body, or even the life of the mind, but the life of the heart. And if Tom's heart tells him that music is what matters most to him, I will support him, gladly, and with all my heart."

Alex, who had been holding the microphone for her father, nodded. Out of the corner of her eye, she saw Marcy pump the air with her fist. She supposed that meant that Coach had come through with what Marcy wanted.

"Thanks, Coach," said Alex, and with her eyes she told him just how much she meant it.

"That's a wrap!" shouted Marcy, and everyone clapped and cheered.

After the news crew left and Tom, Harley, and Jackson went off to sign CDs for people, Ava found herself alone with Alex. Ava could see the gratitude in her sister's expression.

"Ave," said Alex. "Thanks so much for coming to my rescue there. I don't know if I would have recovered from the shock if you hadn't stepped on my toe when you did."

Ava smiled. "It was no big deal," she said.

"And to think I ever thought that Luke—"

"Hey, Luke!" Ava said loudly, interrupting her. She'd seen him approaching.

Alex stopped abruptly and turned toward him.

"Hey, Alex," he said. "I hope I didn't throw a wrench into the works, asking Harley out on camera."

Alex laughed lightly. "Oh, no, it was totally adorable!" she said.

"Yeah, well, I don't know if you know about it, but for Homecoming, they have a contest every year for who has the best surprise-ask. And I've kind of had a crush on Harley for months and was finally starting to think maybe it was reciprocal, so I took a big chance and asked her." He grinned sheepishly.

Ava whacked him over the head with a rolled-up program. "You sure did take a chance! Lucky for you she said yes."

Alex smiled. "Marcy says she's going to keep that part in the piece," she said. "She thought it was cute too."

Luke grinned and gave her a thumbs-up. "Awesome. Thanks again, Alex."

Alex waited until he was several steps away from them to cover her face with her hands and groan.

CHAPTER FIFTEEN

The following afternoon the girls were in the kitchen, helping get ready for Harley, Jackson, and Luke, who were all coming over to watch the segment air. Their mom and dad were in the living room, arranging chairs in front of the TV.

"Did Marcy tell you exactly what time it would be on?" Ava asked Alex as she dumped popcorn into a big bowl.

"Toward the end of the half hour," Alex replied.

Ava knew her sister well enough to see how nervous she was.

Ava heard a tap at the kitchen door and went to open it. It was Coach Byron, along with

Jamila and Shane. The kids gave Ava a big bear hug, and then dashed past her to pet Moxy, who had jumped up to greet them, her tail wagging wildly.

"Hey, Coach B," said Ava. In all the excitement of preparing for the airing of the news story, Ava had almost forgotten to worry about him.

"Hello, girls," said Coach B. "The kids and I are on our way home, but I just wanted to stop by and thank you for what you did."

Ava darted a look at Alex. What was he talking about?

"Oh, it was nothing," said Alex. "We're just really glad it all worked out!"

"It was a really great thing, and I am much obliged," he insisted, and shook each girl by the hand. "Shay. Mila. Let's go, guys. We have to get home in time to watch the big news story!"

And with another thanks and hugs from the kids, the Hardy family headed out again.

Ava turned to Alex, hands on hips. "What in the world did you do, Al?"

"May I remind you that I am a PR person by training?" said Alex with a sly grin. "I set up a network, like a babysitters' club. When Coach Byron needs a sitter, I send out an all-points bulletin to everyone, and the first to respond gets to sit for him. Lindsey heard about it from the captain of the Briar Ridge cheer team—they're doing the same thing for a teacher at their school who has three kids and whose husband's been deployed overseas. I told Daddy about this, and he's going to put off that conversation he had been dreading having with Coach Byron."

Ava regarded her sister with newfound admiration. "That's amazing, Alex."

The front doorbell rang, and they heard Tommy's friends arrive. Their mom yelled to them to come watch.

In the living room, Jackson, Harley, and Luke were wedged onto the couch alongside Tommy, and Coach was fiddling with the remote, setting up the TV to record.

"They just said it would be on after this commercial break," said Mrs. Sackett. The two girls sat down in the chairs Coach had arranged side by side. Mrs. Sackett sat next to Coach on the love seat, holding his hand and beaming already.

Finally a commercial for a car dealership ended, and Marcy Maxon's smile flashed on the screen. "And next, we have our popular feature 'Tomorrow's Reporters Today' for you. Here to share her story is a seventh grader from Ashland Middle School, Alex Sackett."

"Hey, she just called me Alex!" said Alex. "Finally."

Ava found Alex's hand and grabbed it, squeezing tight with excitement.

Alex's image flashed on-screen, and everyone cheered, quickly, and then hushed up to listen.

Ava marveled at how poised and photogenic Alex appeared. She really was a natural.

Alex introduced herself as an identical twin with an older brother, an artist mother, and a father whom most viewers would know as the head coach of the Ashland Tigers. In a voice-over, with Alex narrating, Ava saw footage of Coach coaching, a picture from Mrs. Sackett's website showing her holding up a large vase, Tommy standing in uniform on the sidelines, and a photo of herself in her football uniform. Back to Alex, who smiled charmingly at the camera and talked about her brother's "double life."

The next shot showed the trio playing one of their jazziest pieces and then Alex introducing the other members of the group. Then, in a voice-over, she added, "And Harley has one especially ardent fan." There was a shot of

Luke holding out flowers and asking Harley to Homecoming.

Tommy whapped Luke over the head with a throw cushion, but everyone kept watching. Alex's voice asked, "And who do you think named the trio?" Next Ava appeared on-screen, suggesting her idea.

Finally Alex's voice said, "But what we're all really wondering is, how does the head coach of the Ashland football team feel about his only son potentially choosing music over football?" And then Coach delivered his little speech. Alex closed with, "This has been Alex Sackett for 'Tomorrow's Reporters Today.' Back to you, Marcy!"

Almost immediately, the house phone began ringing, and Ava's cell phone began vibrating with multiple texts—she'd check those later. The high schoolers all let out a loud whoop and stood up from the couch in unison, high-fiving and hugging one another and then taking turns hugging Alex. Ava noticed that Alex remained cool and calm as she accepted a congratulatory hug from Luke. Maybe she really was over him already.

Finally it was Ava's turn to hug Alex. "You

were fantastic," she said to her sister. "I'm really proud to be your sister." And she realized that all her resentment toward what Alex had done was gone. She meant what she said.

CHAPTER SIXTEEN

Later that night Alex came into Ava's room. Ava was sprawled on her bed, working on an essay for English. Alex carefully moved some of the papers out of the way and then plopped onto the bed. "Thanks again for rescuing my story," she said to Ava. "I didn't think you'd show up."

Ava shrugged. "I almost didn't. But when I got home, I found Coach working in the backyard, and I asked him to bring me. I knew he was dying to hear the performance, so I told him about how he could listen from offstage without being seen and causing a fuss."

"I think Tommy was happy, don't you?"

Tommy suddenly loomed in the doorway. He

seemed to be growing at the rate of an inch a week, Alex thought as she regarded him.

"Luke posted our new song just before the story aired, and it's already going viral!" he said. "And he says he's getting flooded with booking requests as far out as next spring!"

The girls looked at each other and in unison gave a big squeal of excitement.

Tommy moved into the room and gathered both girls into a bear hug, scattering Ava's papers all over the floor.

"By the way, Al," said Tommy, as he released them and began gathering the papers, "sorry about the whole Luke thing. I had no clue you liked him, you big goof. If I'd known, I would have told you he liked Harley. And that she's a senior."

"So Luke's into older women, not younger ones," said Ava.

"Whatever. I'm totally over him," said Alex, and she meant it. "I talked with Emily a little while ago, and she says Greg Fowler still hasn't worked up the nerve to ask her to Homecoming, even though everyone can see from a million miles away that he likes her."

Ava and Tommy exchanged amused looks.

"So a bunch of us are all going together," said Alex. "Which reminds me." She stood up. "I have to go finish my to-do chart for Homecoming planning. I'm way behind because of the news story."

She left. Tommy and Ava looked at each other.

"A 'to-do chart'?" he repeated. "For a dance? Are you *sure* she's our sister?"

Ava smiled. "I'm sure."

Ready for more
ALEX AND AVA?

Turn the page for a sneak peek at the
next book in the **It Takes Two** series:

IT TAKES
TWO

May the Best
Twin Win
by Belle Payton

7

"Hey, Emily! Hey, Lindsey!" Alex Sackett waved at her two friends, who were weaving their way through the crowded hallway in her direction. "Wow, they look super excited about something!" Alex said to her twin sister, Ava, whose locker was right next to hers.

Ava grinned and slammed her locker closed before the clutter inside could spill out. "Whatever it is, I'm sure it's important, like a sale on make-up," she joked, hoisting her backpack onto her shoulder. She was already thinking about her first-period Spanish class, and wondering if she had her homework with her. Had she left it at home?

"Don't joke. It probably has to do with Homecoming!" said Alex.

Emily Campbell and Lindsey Davis stopped on either side of Ava and linked arms with her.

"Ava! Just the girl we wanted to see!" said Emily breathlessly.

Alex frowned.

This sudden attention alarmed Ava, but she tried to make a joke out of it. "Uh, hi guys. I realize that Alex and I are identical twins and all, but she's the twin you want to see," she said.

"What? No! I mean, no offense, Alex," said Lindsey, barely glancing at Alex. "But actually, it's you we were coming to find, Ava, because we want to make sure you're signing up for the big game."

"What big game?" asked the twins at the exact same time.

"The Powder Puff football game?" prompted Emily, as though it were the most obvious thing in the world. And Ava noticed that even though Alex had also asked, Emily still addressed her response to Ava.

"Powder what?" asked Ava. This did not sound like something she'd be interested in.

"I know what it is," Alex jumped in. "It's a

flag football game, and it's all girls," she said. "We talked about it in student government on Monday. Next Wednesday, the seventh grade girls play one game and the eighth grade girls play another. Then the winning seventh and eighth grade teams play each other at the big pep rally on Friday. It's a Homecoming thing they do every year to raise money for the local soup kitchen."

Ava could see where this was going. No wonder Emily and Lindsey were interested in her, not Alex. Alex was not known for her athletic prowess, whereas Ava was the one and only girl on the Ashland Middle School football team.

"Do they have to call it 'Powder Puff?'" asked Ava, wrinkling her nose. "That sounds so last century."

Lindsey laughed. "It's just the traditional name for it. But trust me: it's a serious game. We always raise a ton of money."

"And it won't interfere with your football," Emily added quickly. "We only have one practice, this Sunday afternoon."

"This is going to be so fun!" Alex chimed in brightly. "For once I'll get to be on the same team as my twin!" Ava knew that tone of her sister's—Alex was feeling left out.

Ava noticed that Emily and Lindsey exchanged a quick look, just a flick of their eyes. She also noticed that Alex didn't seem to have noticed.

"Well, ha-ha," said Emily, "you probably will be," she said to Alex. "Coach Jen appointed Lindz and me to pick one team, and Rosa and Annelise are picking the other."

"We're not the captains or anything," Lindsey added quickly.

"And after people sign up, we flip a coin to see who gets first pick," continued Emily. "Then we just take turns choosing until everyone is on a team. We're getting together tonight to choose the teams and they'll be posted tomorrow morning."

Ava gulped. Would Alex's friends be loyal to Alex and choose Alex, or would they be more interested in choosing talent? Ava thought she knew the answer, and she didn't think Alex was going to be very happy about it.

"The signup sheets are outside the gym," said Emily to Ava. "Don't forget!"

"I won't," said Ava.

"I won't either!" added Alex. But Emily and Lindsey were already hurrying away.

Alex turned to Ava and frowned. "Should we sign up now? The first bell hasn't rung yet."

Ava shrugged. "I guess."

They found the signup sheets just where Emily had said they'd be. The seventh grade sheet already had fourteen names on it. Ava smiled when she saw that her friend Kylie McClaire had signed up. Kylie had hated football when Ava first met her, but after spending a few of the high school games in the bleachers next to Ava, she now liked it almost as much as Ava did. Ava liked to think it was all thanks to her influence that Kylie now wanted to play on the Powder Puff team.

Ava scrawled her name just below Alex's neatly-penned name.

"Are you sure you have time for this?" asked Alex, pursing her lips. "You know you need to keep your grades up."

Ava scowled at her sister. "Thanks for your concern. I think I can handle one Sunday practice and a couple of Powder Puff games without flunking out," she said irritably. But deep down, she knew her sister had a point. She had been diagnosed with ADHD at the beginning of the school year, and she'd been working extra hard to keep her grades up ever since. She had a big science test on Monday that she really needed to do well on, because she was in danger of getting a C. That could land her on academic probation and jeopardize her ability to play on the AMS football team—the real football team.

But she had a plan. Today was only Thursday. Her tutor, Luke, was making a special visit to her house tonight to help her with test-taking strategies. She'd study all weekend and then ace the science test on Monday.

Dinner that night at the Sackett house was quiet. Alex had set places at the table for her brother, Tommy, and for her dad, but they were late coming back from practice. The twins' father was the coach of the high school football team, the Ashland Tigers, and Tommy was the third-string quarterback.

"We'd better start," said Mrs. Sackett to the girls. "Luke will be here to tutor Ava at 7:30."

Thinking about Luke made Alex's face grow hot, so she looked down intently at the vegetarian taco she was assembling. She couldn't believe how out of control her mad crush on him had gotten! What had she been thinking? Not that he wasn't totally gorgeous, and smart, and funny—in short, a perfect match for her. But he was a sophomore in high school, just like Tommy. Alex knew now that that was too old for her. Whatever. She was pretty sure Luke hadn't noticed how much she'd fawned over him—boys were oblivious at any age, it seemed.

"Have you heard what the committee decided the dress code for Homecoming will be?" Alex asked Ava, as Ava handed her a plate of black beans. "'Snappy casual.' What is that supposed to mean?"

Ava shrugged without looking up from the large taco she was constructing. "You know me, Al. I never let these things bother me. I have you to help me avoid any fashion don'ts."

Alex eyed Ava's football jersey and sniffed. "Well, I wish you'd listen to me a little more often," she chided her sister. "Anyway, I'll do some research about this and find out what people mean by 'snappy casual.'"

"I'll be anxiously awaiting word from you," said Ava.

They heard the front door burst open and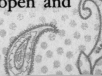

suddenly Tommy loomed in the kitchen door-way. *Did he grow another inch since I saw him this morning?* Alex wondered. Their Australian shepherd, Moxy, who had been slumbering on top of Alex's feet under the table, scrambled to her feet and barreled into him, her tail wagging like crazy.

Coach slipped past his son and dog and bent down to kiss Mrs. Sackett on the cheek.

"Sorry we're late, honey," he said, plunking down his oversized leather briefcase and step-ping to the sink to wash up. Alex was always amazed at how well the orange Tigers coaching shirt complimented his skin tone—how was that possible, for such a bright, garish color? Maybe it was the deep Texas tan he'd acquired in the few months since they'd moved there.

"Are you ready for the game tomorrow?" asked Mrs. Sackett as she playfully slapped Tommy, who was attempting to sit down, and pointed at the sink for him to wash his hands.

"It's going to be an easy one, right, Coach?" asked Ava.

"There are no 'easy ones' in this league, Ava," said Coach.

"Well, easier, then," amended Ava.

Alex didn't know football the way her sister did, but she'd known their dad long enough to know that he never conceded that a game could be easy. She supposed this was a coach thing.

"It's the Homecoming game next week we have to worry about," said Coach. "We have to beat Western if we want any chance to make it to State."

"Oh, I am so excited for Homecoming Week!" said Alex, bouncing up and down a little in her chair. "I can't believe the dance is a week from Saturday! So, Tommy, are you going to the high school dance with a big group?"

Tommy had built himself three towering tacos in a remarkably short time. He picked up the first one, his mouth open wide, but stopped before he took a bite and said, "No. I'm thinking of asking someone." Then half the taco disappeared.

The other four Sacketts stopped and stared at him.

Alex recovered first. "You're going to ask a girl?"

Tommy swallowed and glared at her. "No, it's actually a pet armadillo," he said, and made the rest of the taco disappear.

This was big news. Tommy was supercute and Alex knew lots of girls were interested in him, but to her knowledge, he'd never really reciprocated any of their interest. Or at least, if he had, he had never talked about it.

Tommy was funny and playful and pretty nice about driving Alex and Ava places when they asked, but he didn't share much about his love life.

"Who is it?" demanded Ava. "Anyone we know?"

So this is news to Ava, too, Alex thought. She was glad. Sometimes she felt a little jealous of the close bond her brother and sister shared.

"He'll tell us when he's ready," said Mrs. Sackett, with a glance at Coach. "Tom, honey, you're acting like you haven't eaten in three days. You don't have to eat quite so fast. I'm afraid you'll choke."

Tommy had already polished off two tacos and was starting on the third. "I've got rehearsal in twenty minutes," he said.

Tommy also played piano in a jazz trio in the little time off he had from football. Alex smiled. His group had gotten tons of attention recently, ever since she'd done a feature story about them for the "Tomorrow's Reporters Today" segment on the local news.

"I need to get ready for Luke," said Ava, pushing her chair back from the table. "I have a big, huge, important science test on Monday."

"I think it's wonderful that you're applying yourself so much, honey," said Mrs. Sackett.

Alex jumped up and helped her brother and sister clear the table. "I need to go, too," she said. "I'm going to ransack my closet to see what items qualify as 'snappy casual'—that's the dress code for our Homecoming dance—so I can do an inventory of possibilities."

Tommy grinned. "You do that, Al. And be sure to start a spreadsheet so we can run the numbers later."

Alex knew Tommy was teasing her, but that was okay. He was never a mean teaser.

Mrs. Sackett sighed and put a hand over her husband's. "Well, we did enjoy five minutes of overlap when all of us were together at the dinner table. Not bad for the middle of football season."

Belle Payton isn't a twin herself, but she does have twin brothers! She spent much of her childhood in the bleachers reading—er, cheering them on—at their football games. Though she left the South long ago to become a children's book editor in New York City, Belle still drinks approximately a gallon of sweet tea a week and loves treating her friends to her famous homemade mac-and-cheese. Belle is the author of many books for children and tweens and is currently having a blast writing two sides to each It Takes Two story.

sew zoey

If you think Alex and Ava
are fun, wait until you meet
Zoey Webber, a seventh grader
turned fashion blogger!
Check out the Sew Zoey books,
available at your favorite store!